AF482024

This project is dedicated to all of the polymaths and blerds who can't make up their minds.

Don't.

TABLE OF CONTENTS

This book is important to me.

I am a polymath.

Polymath
/'pälē,maTH/
noun
a person of wide-ranging knowledge or learning.

My latest book is called Smush. I named this project Smush because I smushed all of the facets of my art into one book. I crammed poetry, photography, recipes, open letters, and bits of advice, all layered over a foundation of four short stories.

The short stories in Smush are the newest adventure for me. A while ago, I expressed dissatisfaction in the stories that we told about and by people of color. I wanted new stories that didn't start from a deficit model, and I had a hard time finding them.

Toni Morrison sad, "If there's a book that you want to read, but it hasn't been written yet, then you must write it.," so I wrote the stories that I wanted to read. Four of them. I am so very proud of these four stories, and I want to share them with the world.

Smush is a different kind of book. It makes perfect sense to me and to polymaths like myself. Stuff everywhere, all at once, jammed next to each other. Smush feels like a warm sweater on a chilly fall day in the northeast of part of country to me, but I know that not everyone's mind works that way. I recognized that it might be helpful to separate the stories out and give them their own room to breathe. "Smush: Just Shorts" is that breathing room.

Happy reading.

PORTAL....

<h1 style="text-align:center">Chapter 1</h1>

Vero hated the water. Sure. Oceans, Lakes, and Mountain streams were a great backdrop but solid ground was her thing. Trees, rocks, and things she could climb were more in tune with her sensibilities. Not flat, placid water that stretched for miles to the horizon.

Yet, here she was, in a village floating on a massive lake in the middle of nowhere in Thailand. No trees. No rocks. Lots of water. This was not the trip she thought she had signed up for a while back. Too fluid of a soul to actually read an itinerary, Vero thought a trip to Thailand would involve far more majestic views from smoky mountain tops. Instead, she had just spent the night floating. On water. Flat, placid, water.

An early riser, Vero was up long before the rest of the women on the trip. She needed to center herself. The widest pieces of the solid surface were attached to the house where they were staying. It was the floating dock where the long tail boats would pull up to make deliveries from the nearest town. At 4:30 a.m., it was deserted and perfectly quiet for Vero's morning walk, albeit far shorter than she was used to walking.

As she neared the edge of the dock, wearing just a sarong wrapped around her naked body, she was thankful that she was able to snatch this small bit of freedom. Clothing choices were limited in Thailand and for a person who loved to feel the air on as much of her skin, being covered up in such a beautifully warm climate seemed doubly cruel. That's why being outside, draped in nothing but a thin sarong was a glorious act of personal rebellion.

The edge of the dock reminded her that it was a small freedom. She stood there, staring at the rest of the houses gently bobbing in concert with each other on the murky lake and she wondered what actually lay below her in that water. It was a brownish shade of green and as opaque as a liquid could be before being described as a sludge. Who knows what was hiding down there?

Vero plopped down and centered her thoughts, trying to meditate herself back to a higher altitude in her thoughts and a higher consciousness. All she could hear in her mind was the yoga instructor from the excursion two days ago, whose voice was distracting at best. He was ridiculous and kept telling them to align their chakras and to "focus on your sexual organs." It's hard enough to focus in a warrior pose without being asked to think about your vagina while doing it! Nonetheless, Vero found herself sitting on that dock and starting to focus on her womb, all in the heavy Indian accent of the yoga instructor. The voice kept saying to be still. Go deeper. Focus.

She could start to feel her body relax and her thoughts about the future capabilities of her womb flooded her mind. The more she focused, the warmer her organs seemed to feel. This began to confuse Vero, so she concentrated even more. Deeper. More focus. And then... she was... gone.

Chapter 2

Click was killing it. A night owl and the group's resident nerd and techno-geek, she had heard Vero stir from across the room and grabbed her handheld gaming system, and started a new set. Like Vero, Click was not happy on the lake. She heard Thailand with her girls and images of nights in Bangkok were all she could think of. She sent the full payment to the travel agent long before they even crafted an agenda. That's why she was a bit taken aback when she ended up way south of the bustling main city, sleeping on a mat in a house floating peacefully on a lake. It didn't matter though, as long as she had her girls and her personal tech, she was having fun.

Most of the time. She had a different idea as to what she would be doing at 5:00 a.m. in Thailand though. Mostly she anticipated that she would be stumbling back from a burlesque show where the performer's gender was undetermined at 5:00 a.m. Or scoring some weird drug that was only available in the dark streets of the city. Sunrises on a lake weren't in the picture. Click was glad they were though. She had needed this. Click lived in Vegas and, although her neighborhood wasn't as glitzy as the Strip, fast times were always virtually around the corner. Plus she was a major stakeholder in an Esports company, so she was always around throngs of screaming Asian people. Bangkok would have felt like more of the same. This was a welcomed departure, even if it was unintentional.

Click wondered where Vero was as she dominated yet another level of a game that her company had gotten a pre-release copy of before it hit the market. Click and Vero were thick as thieves in college. In fact, it was Vero that gave Click her nickname. She would be up at ungodly hours, clicking away at video games in their dorm room. Someone asked Vero how her roommate was at lunch one day and she responded, "Who? The Late Night Clicker?" The name stuck and before long it got back to Click whose real name was Marigold. At first, Click was furious that her roommate was talking about her behind her back. Click thought that they were cool and she viewed this as a betrayal of their friendship. After they talked it out, Vero explained that the constant clicking of the game controller and the keyboard late at night was a constant imposition, which was new information for Click. They patched up their spat and then Click revealed that she hated the name Marigold. It literally made her sound like the child of flower children and nothing could be further from the truth about her family. Both Click's parents were lawyers, one corporate and one public defendant. They were very heady people, but when they had a daughter, they went with a very nonprofessional name. In actuality, it was the name of the first client for whom her mother won a case for. It was a poignant memory for Click's mom. It was less than impactful as a computer science major and coder. What was even worse for the "then Marigold" was when people shortened her name to "Ma-ree." It implied an assumed comfort level from the person doing the shortening that was generally incorrect and mostly unsolicited. She may not have liked her name, but she disliked people who took liberties with it even more. When Marigold found out that people were referring to her as "The Clicker" and sometimes as Click, she was secretly ok with it. It spoke to her true self far more than her given name. When it was out in the open that she knew about the moniker and she had her "come to Jesus" talk with Vero, she let it be known that it was actually fine to refer to her as Click. Something changed in her when she adopted the name Click. There was a kind of rebirth in her mind. Her introductions went from sheepish "Marigold" with a bowed head, to an emphatic, "Click" with chest puffed and extended hand. She felt like a superhero with a hidden identity and secret abilities. It was empowering and it changed her persona in ways she did not anticipate. She did the obligatory big chop with her hair which is almost mandatory when a woman experiences a change in their life. She immediately regretted it. It was so cliché and the style didn't suit her. It was a lesson learned, and she re-grew her hair, added a little color to it, and logged the fact that nothing is permanent on her mental database. The new look from the haircut garnered her the attention of people who she had not met before and suddenly her social circle swelled, all because of a click.

Click put her device down and headed out of the room towards the attached dock. She was confident that she had heard Vero come out this way, but now there was no sign of her. The sun was now up so she had a clear view of the entire dock. There weren't very many things to hide behind on the bamboo platform and even fewer hiding spots with the light of the early morning. Vero wasn't there and panic set in Click's mind. They were surrounded by greenish murky river water. Taking an early morning dip was not an option here. These waterways were primarily for transportation and although in the early afternoon you could see the village children playing in the water, Vero and company's westerner sensibilities and immunities were not a good match for this opaque viscous liquid. In fact, if Vero had fallen in somehow, there is a good chance that western sensibility would have caused anxiety and ensuing disaster. This was the source of Click's panic.

She walked to the edge of the dock, each step diminishing her hope of good news. Maybe an early morning fisherman came by and offered to show Vero around. Perhaps she had found a way to climb onto the roof of the home. Could she have tried to be brave and followed the example of the village children and actually gotten into the water? Click's mind was racing and at the very least, she hoped for a note. Or a sign. Or a message.

There was nothing.

Once she realized that there was no doubt that Vero was not on the floating structure, she hastened back to the inner room. There were no interior walls so there was no chance that Vero was in the room and somehow Click had missed her. She was gone and it was officially time to worry. Click woke everyone up as gently and as urgently as she could. First, she woke Joseph and Claudia, which was always tricky. They were borderline exhibitionists so you never knew the state of undress you were going to find them in at any given time. Fortunately, this time they were fully clothed and disentangled.

"Joe. I think Vero is missing," whispered Click, shaking him to give him confirmation that she wasn't part of his dream.

"Huh," he muttered. "Where are we?"

It was a fair question. This trip took them to several locations and they laid their heads in multiple beds over the course of the last week. It took Click a few moments each morning to get her bearings, so she understood Joe's disorientation.

"In the water village. I can't find Vero."

The fog from Joseph's thoughts began to clear and his firefighter training kicked in. It was interesting to see him go from groggy and half asleep to a fully alert, first responder. That is if Click was in the mental place to notice that.

"How do you know?"

"I thought I heard her get up and walk outside and I thought I would go keep her company. When I got out there, the dock was empty and I don't see her anywhere. We're in a floating house, so there aren't many options. I don't know where she could be."

Without giving a response, Joseph jumped up and went to check the dock for himself, with Click in tow. He surveyed the exact same spots that Click had. At that moment, she was comforted that he had done the same things that she had and annoyed that he was doing things that she had already told him were covered. She physically shook her head to shake those thoughts: now is not the time to be annoyed by a man not trusting a woman's assessment of the situation. Vero was missing and a second set of eyes couldn't hurt.

"Well she is definitely not out here," he mansplained. "Do you remember whether there was a rowboat or something out here before? Maybe she went for a solo boat ride?"

"I thought of that but I think I would have heard the paddle splashes if she did. When she walked out here, it woke me up and I've been up since then. Where the hell could she be?"

"I don't know. Let's wake everyone up."

By now the sun was coming up and some of the group had begun to stir. Claudia was sitting straight up, doing stretches. She gave Joseph an 'Oh there you are' look as he entered the room which quickly changed to a quizzical one when Click followed right behind him. It was clear that she hadn't heard Click wake Joseph up and she had only stirred when her cuddle partner was missing. Click recognized that look quickly and immediately spoke to squash any suspicions.

"Everyone get up. We can't find Vero. I woke up early and couldn't find her. I woke Joe up and he couldn't find her either."

Click watched as Claudia's face softened with relief that her man wasn't being inappropriate and then tensed back up as the fact that Vero was missing sunk in. The rest of the group of eight, as well as their guide and host family, jumped up with the news and started to scramble. The father of the host family got a quick translation from their guide and immediately scampered outside. Click followed him as he followed the same search pattern that she and Joe had used. Then, without hesitation, he dove into the murky green water at the back of the house. A few moments later, he re-emerged near the front only to dive back in to search the other side. He surfaced again and shook his head to our guide, signaling that he hadn't found anything. Click tried to convince herself that that was a good thing and that it meant Vero hadn't fallen off and got caught under the structure. Click's inner mind wasn't buying it though.

Their guide moved everyone back into the floating house and while their host toweled off, he started to get the details of exactly what had happened. When did they last see Vero? Did she say anything to anyone? Is she prone to disappearing and wandering off? Could she swim? As their guide continued his interrogation, they heard footsteps.

"There is someone outside!" yelled Joe, as he raced out the door. The entire group emptied out of the house behind him and stopped dead in their tracks in a semicircle. In front of them, was a bewildered-looking Vero, stark naked and trembling. Just before she collapsed on the deck, she mumbled,

"What day is it?"

Chapter 3

Patty nearly passed out. She and Vero lived together back home and Vero was her closest friend, even though that friendship wasn't equally reciprocated. Patty and Vero were sorority sisters and even though they were unevenly yoked in their friendship, Vero loved her. They had gone through a lot together and even their current living situation was a result of trauma. When Patty was jarred from her slumber in her sleeping bag by the announcement that Vero was missing, she froze. A fatalist at heart, she at once presumed the worst, and her mind raced as she tried to figure out what her life would be without her Vero. As their host ran out the door and she heard him splashing about, she remained frozen. As he came back in and she saw Joe's glum face, she remained frozen. Even as the room emptied to see what was making the footstep noises outside, she remained frozen. Patty's mind had buried her friend, begun to mourn, and was starting to formulate a world in which Vero did not exist. It took all of her energy and left none to supply motion to her body. She was the last one left in the house and that realization gut-punched her back to the present day. She followed her friends outside and saw her naked friend, alive and well in front of her. She did not know how to process this situation. Her mind had already moved on.

She was in mourning already. Now here was Vero, back from the dead and naked in front of her.

Oh my God. She's naked.

Since she was the last one out of the house, she was the closest to the door, so Patty dashed back into the house and grabbed a throw blanket from her stuff, and rushed back outside. At first, she did not see Vero and she started her panic-induced paralysis again. Then, through the bodies of her friends, she saw Vero crumbled in a heap on the deck. She pushed past everyone and got to Vero at the same time that Click did. She shot a look to say, "I got this," which was coolly returned with one that said, "Not by yourself you don't." Patty draped the blanket over her friend. It gave her just enough coverage to shield most of her intimate areas. Patty did a quick survey and assessed that Vero didn't have any major visible bruises. To be frank, her skin looked amazing, as if she had been exfoliating and had gotten a tan. Patty pondered the impossibility of that as she continued to check her housemate for injuries. Vero had been a whole shade lighter last night. Her tan seemed to have darkened in mere hours. Click seemed to be noticing the same thing. They glanced up at each other, silently agreed on their confusion, and then Vero refocused them on their patient.

"What day is it?" she muttered again.
"It's still Tuesday," Click answered.
"What do you mean 'still?' How long have I been gone?" Vero seemed confused. Just then, Kwame, Joe's friend from college, came over with a bottle of water for Vero. She took it and downed it in seconds. Kwame, Vero, and Click all watched as Vero caught her breath after chugging the water, each bewildered by Vero's last statement.

"Vero. You went missing just this morning according to Click. What happened to you?" inquired Kwame. Click and Patty were visibly annoyed by his intrusion, the way detectives in movies get annoyed when FBI agents poke their noses into their cases. Kwame was sweet on Vero and had spent the entire trip trying to get in good with her and deflecting all of her rebuffs. Click was pissed off that he would use this moment to weasel some attention to himself and redirected Vero's attention.

"Yeah, Vero. You woke up this morning, walked outside, and disappeared. Then just as suddenly, you showed up again. What happened?"

Without blinking, Vero glared at Click and said, in an unwavering voice,

"I was kidnapped."

Chapter 4

Patty leaned in a bit closer to re-establish her position in the melee and, in a way, in Vero's actual life. She didn't like Click's proximity to Vero, neither physically nor metaphorically. Patty didn't trust Click. She viewed her as prone to fancy and wishy-washy behavior. Granted she had stumbled into something major with the e-sports (something Patty didn't fully understand. "So people fill arenas to watch OTHER people play video games?" she once asked) but there was no telling when Click was going to grow bored with it and move on to the next thing that tweaked her interest. That "next thing" could very well be around the globe in Nepal for instance, which is where Click disappeared to when she decided that she needed to "go off the grid" for a minute. That lasted six months. In fact, the very reason they were all in Thailand in a house floating on a lake was because Click suggested that they should throw caution to the wind. Click lived in Vegas and seemed to crave excitement so she suggested that they should go somewhere interesting for Connie's 30th birthday. Connie, Vero's younger sister Consuela, lit up when she heard the idea, however, it was clear that her idea of a Thailand trip was very different from what Click had in mind, or Vero for that matter. Click spent most of her time with her nose buried in one device or another and Vero and Connie bickered the entire time. Connie probably thought that this "disappearance" was some stunt to draw attention to Vero which is why she wasn't front and center at her sister's re-appearance.

Patty blamed all of it on Click, directly and indirectly, and she would have preferred that she was the one closest to Vero, both in this moment and in life. Patty probably would not have been concerned with the way Click lived her life if not for the fact that Vero was drawn to her like a thrill-seeking moth to a recklessly untethered flame. It worried Patty that Vero was so enamored with Click because Click had no inhibitions and, as a result, Vero had no self-control around her. Everything seemed like a good idea to Vero and she didn't have the fortitude that Click had for substances and an aggressive lifestyle. When Click caught a cold, figuratively, Vero came down with pneumonia. It was always Patty, the stable one, that had to pick up the pieces.

Patty wished that Vero wanted to hang out with her with the same frequency that she yearned for Click's company. She knew that she wasn't exciting, but hadn't they had enough excitement? Wasn't it time to call it quits at that stage of their lives?

All of them were career-minded women and had achieved success in their own separate rights. Patty felt that it was time to put the days (and nights) of experimental drug use and anonymous hook-ups behind them.

That lifestyle was what Click represented and it was time to let her go.
"Let her go. Give her some room. She's clearly disoriented," Patty barked at Click.
She hadn't realized that she had meandered deep into her own thoughts and was
not verbalizing in a tone that was inappropriate for the situation. Visibly taken
aback, Click stepped aside, rattled.

"Sorry. Click. I didn't mean it that way. But she just said she was kidnapped.
Vero, honey," turning to her housemate, "What are you talking about? No one
kidnapped you." "But they did. And they have been using me for weeks. You're
telling me that I have only been missing an hour? That can't be!" Vero pleaded her
case.

Vero was shaking now and demonstrably confused. It was obvious that she
believed that something crazy had been done to her and that it didn't line up with
what her friends and family experienced.

"Vero, darling. What do you think happened to you? Tell us and let's see if we can
figure this out," Patty inquired, going into full counselor mode.

"They took me. But it all started with that stupid Indian yogi and his sexual organ
shakra thing!"

Chapter 5

Vero had focused on her sexual organs that morning and that started the trouble.
As she recanted the events of what were the last three weeks for her, the eyes of
everyone around her started to widen in disbelief and confusion. The more she
talked, the less she believed her own tale so she knew this must seem incredulous
to everyone else.

"I went to the dock that morning," she began.

"This morning," interrupted Click.

"Perhaps but for me, that was almost three weeks ago," Vero explained, causing
more stupefied looks.

According to Vero's version of the events, she reached a deeper level of
concentration that morning on the dock. She didn't know if it was because of the

gentle rocking of the floating house or the instructions from the yogi resonating in her head, but she felt her body relax to the point of melting away. Not "away" though, but melting inward towards where her womb was in her lower parts. And then she began to emanate heat again, from the area of her womb. During this experience, she kept her eyes closed. Tightly. She couldn't tell whether she was imagining all of these feelings or if something was actually happening to her body, however, if this is what a deep meditative state felt like, she didn't want to blow it by opening her eyes. From everything that she had ever read about when yogis transcended into this state, her body was supposed to feel like it was floating. Weightlessly. That was not what was happening to her though. The sensation of her body folding into itself through her uterus was intensifying, too much for her to bear and she opened her eyes to a sight she could not previously fathom. Everything around her was vicious and green and seemed to be flowing straight through her at the source of her intense feelings.

She was underwater.

Chapter 6

Almost simultaneously with Vero's submersion, a finned creature was also entering into a meditative state. Her name was Oo. As the leader of her people, Oo was brilliant. The possessor of Solomon-like wisdom, she guided her people for 114 years. They had seen many things during the time of her rule and had enjoyed bounty beyond their wildest dreams. Oo was committed to creating a sanctuary where her species could thrive, away from the prying eyes of humans and their toxic tentacles of pollution. For the most part, she had been successful. When a part of her kingdom was destroyed by the actions of men, they forged deeper into the sea. As the curious humans probed further into the watery depths, Oo's people set up defenses and misdirection to remain undetected. It was becoming increasingly impossible to keep mankind at bay. New technology allowed scientists to probe around every corner of the ocean now and it was only a matter of time before man's next greatest discovery would be Oo's people. She could not let that happen and so, in the fashion of her father, and the leaders that ruled before him, Oo sought advice from the universe. She sank to the floor of the pitch-black waters of the Pacific and began to chant to the ancestors and the universe for answers to problems her people were facing.

Her chanting induced her into a meditative state as she stilled her mind and body. Slowly she became one with the water surrounding her and soon the ocean floated her up off the floor. Oo began to realize that she wasn't just floating. She was moving, with purpose and she slowly opened her eyes and realized she was being pulled toward a murky green glow, barely discernible in the darkness.

At that moment, she made a decision. In her mind, it was clear that this was a sign from the ocean and she should heed it. Rather than be pulled to the emerald glow, Oo began to swim towards it and, as she approached the mysterious point, she realized that it was larger than a point in the abyss. It was the size of the barrel of her chest and quickly she realized that it was a portal. The green glow was murky water on the other side of this door. Oo knew that she had to make a decision: ignore that this was the sign that she had asked for or explore where this portal led. She chose the latter and squeezed through the opening. In doing so, she imagined that this must have been what being born was like: from darkness, through an opening, into a different world.

Oo pulled her entire body through and surveyed her new environment. The water was dense with debris and plant matter. Swimming in it was laborious but it wasn't thick enough to block out light. It had been many decades since her people saw light from the sun. The humans had forced them deeper and deeper into the oceanic trenches and daylight exposure was a rarity. Oo stretched her arms straight up and twirled around to soak up all of the light she could. She was reveling in the refracted sunlight, still twirling, when she came face to face with a human woman. Her shock was equal to the human's astonishment and she tried to attack Oo. Or swim away. Or reach out for help. Regardless of which it was, Oo's natural defenses caused her to grab this woman's wrist and there was a flash of light. Blinding them both, Oo and this human blinked their eyes to readjust. The woman's astonishment did not dissipate. They had both been transported away from the green water where the flash occurred. The confused look on the woman's face was because she did not know where she was after she experienced the flash. Oo was confused as well, but it was because she actually recognized her location.

They were back at her village.

Chapter 7

Vero continued her story. A lot was happening all at once. She had opened her eyes from her meditation to find that she was underwater. More importantly, she wasn't drowning. It wasn't that she could now breathe underwater; she wasn't breathing at all. There was no heave to her chest and her immediate assumption was that she was dead. She did not have time to process that thought because there were other things now happening with her body. The implosive forces that were overwhelming her mere moments previously were now being replaced by an energy exploding from her, without regard for her small frame. The pressure was excruciating and Vero shut her eyes in pain.

Then the pain was over.

Vero opened her eyes, one at a time, to survey her surroundings. Her head had been turned over her right shoulder in pain so when she peeked through her squinted lids, she still saw nothing but green water. She still wasn't breathing and she began to turn her head back towards the front of her body. She had intended to inspect where she had experienced the agony, but she did not get the chance because floating in front of her was a creature that was not there moments before.

Her skin was a deep golden color and her form was humanoid for the most part. Her face had no nose and her mouth stretched from one of the appendages on the side of her head to its match on the other side. Her body looked like an Olympic swimmer; muscular and broad at the shoulders, tapering down as you approached the feet. This being did not have feet though. Instead, its legs flattened out at the ends and resembled oars. She was completely naked but her genitalia was not easily detectable. Even with ambiguous genitalia, Vero's new companion was unmistakably a woman.

This description of the creature Vero later learned was named Oo came much later after the first encounter. She did not have time to survey the being in front of her where vacant water had been seconds before. Her arm shot forward in a motion governed by reflex and fear. Oo responded to her motion and grabbed her arm at the wrist.

Once again, in quick succession, Vero was subjected to tumult. Out of seemingly nowhere, there was a bright flash of light and the feeling that she had been sucked into a vortex. As quickly as it started, it was over and Vero had a new set of circumstances to process…and a new environment to analyze.

She was now in a wholly unfamiliar, wondrous place. It bore no resemblance to anything that she had seen or imagined before. It was the brightest darkness that she had ever witnessed. There was light everywhere, emanating from every surface, it seemed, but it was clear that they were deep underwater. None of the light was the result of proximity to the sun. It all seemed to be luminescent material that covered all of the rocks and structures. And what magnificent structures they were! There were stone arches that looked like they were made from coral, crisscrossing back and forth, each end firmly planted in a dome-like enclosure. The arches formed natural causeways and the largest of them all led directly to the largest dome in the distance. That dome looked as if it were created from a combination of smaller ones. Vero would later come to find out that that was the center of the village and the main dome was like the city center. Each of the smaller domes it was composed of, was a domicile for one of the chief's advisors or staff. It was very similar to a bee's honeycomb in functionality. Vero barely had any time to soak in the majesty of this new place before both this new creature and her were swarmed by throngs of beings from the domes. They all looked like versions of Oo and they clamored around her in celebration. She seemed taken aback by the adulation for some reason or perhaps she was still woozy like Vero from being whisked around.

She could not hear sounds but it was clear that town people had gasped at the sight of her. At that moment Vero self-assessed and realized why they were astonished. She was twice their size, her appendages ended in funny-looking toe-like things, and she was glowing. Vera realized she was glowing, but not all over, just in her center area. Remarkably, amidst all of this craziness, Vero managed to smile as she remembered a scene from the movie Harlem Nights. Apparently, her vagina had turned into sunshine, she thought. That would be the last time she would laugh about the glow that she was producing. The very last time.

Chapter 8

Oo's entire village was coming out to greet her. Apparently, they had seen a flash and suddenly she had appeared holding the hand of a giant glowing woman. They all rushed to them because they knew that she had gone to commune with the spirits for an answer to their situation. Here she was now with what seemed to be a goddess. In their eyes, prayers had been answered. It was obvious that their leader had reached out and brought forth the one who would save them.

Oo quieted the crowd. She was as confused by the events as her villagers were. She needed counsel. But first, she needed to assess this human. Oo was one of the few people in her village that had ever seen a human and all of the stories that had been passed down to her described them as aggressive. To this point, she had not shown signs that she was going to attack but that could be because she was stunned from her being magically transported to this village. At any moment, she could go on a rampage and try to destroy the village in an effort to escape. The villagers all looked at her like she was a deity. They had never seen a human before. Oo had and she had a healthy skepticism about this woman. She had never encountered a glowing human though. In addition to their brute strength and size difference, which always posed an issue to their settlements, this human may have different destructive powers as well. Oo had to play this precisely or her entire colony could be in danger. First things first, she had to figure out a way to communicate with her.

She waved her arms in what she hoped was a welcoming fashion and prayed that one of the things that her people and humans had in common was an understanding of a gesture of greeting. Her plan was to get this glowing giant to follow her while she sought out Plesu. Plesu was the oldest among them and the keeper of the tribe's oral history. If there was an explanation for what was happening, Plesu would have it. At least, that is what Oo hoped. Frankly, she had spent many a morning literally at the fins of Plesu and he had never mentioned a glowing human before. In Oo's mind, that was pretty significant and if she hadn't heard of a story like it before, it probably was the first time it happened.

Oo didn't have to go far to find the elder. As she was attempting to coax the woman closer to the village, the crowd was parting behind her, Plesu was making his way to the source of the commotion. Over her shoulder, Oo could see her sage approaching her and breathed a sigh of relief. Even as the leader of her people, and like most rulers, there were gaps in her knowledge.

This is the reason that most heads of state have an advisory council. In this particular situation, Oo knew that she was in over her head and she was happy to see her trusted advisor. Her joy turned to confusion as Plesu's face transformed into pure wonderment and he uttered the words,
"You found a Portal!"

Chapter 9

On the dock, Click had begun to pace. Vero's story was getting wilder and crazier with each passing moment. The group members were beginning to look like they believed that she was having some sort of psychological break. Especially Patty. Ever the pragmatist, Patty had long suppressed her ability to believe in the unexplainable and was solely reliant on logic and scientific method. Although she was raised as a devout Catholic, life had given her a different appreciation of the mysteries of life and now she described herself as agnostic. Vero's story had one explanation in Patty's counselor mind: something had snapped in her mind and this was the beginning of a break from reality.

Click's understanding of this tale was quite different. She was a student of the mystic. While everyone was moaning, groaning, and giggling at the Indian yogi, Click was totally into it. It was right up her alley. The mysticism of true yoga was a passion of hers. Chakras. Transcendence. Meditative states leading to levitation. The whole thing. She believed that it was a possibility and that if you opened your consciousness enough, there was no limit to the power of the human mind. Click also was a fan of science fiction and for her, it was less fiction and more predictive text. She believed that aliens were real. She believed that spirits were real. She believed that robots and AI were already running around. She knew in her heart that there was so much more than the observable world. There had to be. The world was way too boring for this to be it.

As Vero continued with her story, the level of disbelief that her friends were feeling was matched by how much Click was into it. This is what she had been waiting for. Confirmation that there was more. Vero was the 'more'. All this time, it was Vero. Click wanted to push all of the non-believers to the side and have Vero speak directly to her. But that wasn't an option so she settled for leaning in intently.

"Right as I realized that I was glowing," Vero was talking again, "the chica that had transported me to the village was motioning me to come closer to her. Every bone in my body was telling me to swim away."

Vero started to do just that and then she spotted the older gentleman over Oo's shoulder and he had the kindest eyes that she had ever seen, on a human or sea creature. Later, she would come to know that those kind eyes belong to the elder named Plesu. He had such a regal, wise way about him that it took her breath away. And then she realized something quite significant: she was still not breathing. Still no heave and fall rhythm to her chest but she wasn't suffocating either. Yet, there she was, underwater. Not dying. With a glowing vagina. It was all very disorienting which is probably why she decided to move towards Plesu when he beckoned for her to follow him. He seemed to have answers somehow. There was wisdom in his eyes and perhaps he could shed some light on all of this craziness.

When she reached Plesu, Vero took his hand and a surge of energy coursed through her body. It was nothing like the abrupt shock that preceded her being transported here. This was warm and inviting, like Plesu's eyes. It reassured her that this elder could be trusted. There was more though. This same energy seemed to be a conduit for their thoughts. When Plesu turned to the tribe and spoke to them in order to calm their fears, she couldn't understand what he said. When he shifted his gaze to her and explained what he had just said, she understood everything telepathically. Plesu explained that his people had not seen a human for many generations. His village actively avoided their destructive nature, a sentiment that resonated with Vero. The village that they were in was many leagues below the surface and highly camouflaged from both humans and predatory sea creatures. He explained that even with that level of separation, humans were developing technology that would soon be able to peer into corners of the ocean that were previously unattainable. This is why their leader, Oo, had attempted to commune with the spirits and find a solution. That is what had brought them together.

Oo, who had never left Vero's side, was getting a play-by-play from Plesu verbally as he sent his thoughts to Vero. She looked as confused as Vero by all of this. Just then Plesu, seemingly tired of translating his own thoughts and words, paused and excused himself. He moved to the edge of the courtyard that they were standing in and began to chant. Vero still couldn't make out the words that he used but gradually she started to hear a low murmur under his voice that was getting louder. And louder. And clearer. Vero realized that his thoughts were now coming at the same time as his words. It sounded like when you hear a foreign diplomat talking at the United Nations but the translator's voice is louder.

"This is better," Plesu said/thought. "I remember reading a ritual that spoke about this. I always thought it was fantasy but clearly the circumstances today dictate that we open our minds to many possibilities. This way I can speak to you both simultaneously. I will tell Oo anything you think and do the same for her. Now it's time for me to tell you both about a legend that may explain why you are here Vero. You have been brought here to save us all."

<h1 style="text-align:center">Chapter 10</h1>

This was beginning to anger Oo. She had spent an inordinate amount of time learning about her people and their past. She had been groomed as the successor to her childless uncle for as long as she could remember. Never did Plesu mention that there was a story that he didn't want to tell her. Her growing anger stemmed from being unprepared. Plesu knew that Oo was about to meditate in order to connect with the spirits. It would have been helpful to know that there was a possibility of this happening, even if it was a far-fetched fable. This took her by surprise and she appeared to be just as confused as the people who were her subjects. Oo was embarrassed and that embarrassment was leading to her anger.

Still, this was knowledge that she needed. She would deal with Plesu and the omission later. Right now, her priority was to be attentive. Apparently, this human woman was the key to their survival.

Somehow, Plesu had created a psychic link with the woman and was relaying information to both of them, acting as a translator. Her name was Vero and it seemed that this mysticism was a new concept for her as well. When Plesu left to chant alone, Oo surveyed the newest guest to the village. Her distrust for humans was well-founded in lore and in experience. The lore was passed down to her by the elders like Plesu who spoke of a time when her people lived closer to the surface in shallow underwater caves. Human curiosity led them to their settlements and, as with most things that the surface dwellers didn't understand, they tried to catch them for novelty and experimentation. Their sighting spurred on the mermaid legend and her people quickly learned to keep as far away from probing eyes and fingers. Increasingly, that became harder to do. Some of the previous generations had gone on the offensive and slain random divers who got too close. Just in case.

Oo's experience with the humans was more environmental as the pollutants that they dumped into the oceans made it inhabitable for her village, forcing them to move at least twice. Coupled with new technology, Oo had a healthy distrust for the humans and their effect on her tribe. That included the one floating in her village courtyard.

Plesu had begun to speak to them.

"Many generations ago, our people were in tune with the universe. We lived both on land and in the sea and moved seamlessly from one to the other. We also moved from ocean to sea to river and the like with no complications. It was all done through portals, tears in the fabric of the world that connected time and space. Sometimes these portals were spots on the reef or
hidden on a field or on the bank of a river. Some were stationary and permanent, while others moved from place to place. Some portals were allegedly people. Legend has it that there were those in each tribe that vibrated in harmony with the portals and could find them even if they were moving. This story was lost to time because there has never been any evidence that this was true. We live for hundreds of years and no elder has ever seen a portal nor had any of the elders that they studied with. We passed it off as a way of explaining why there were tribes in far-flung oceans, where migration would have been very difficult in ancient times." As Plesu spoke, she glanced at Vero to gauge how she was processing all of this. Her face reflected how Oo was feeling. It was clear that Plesu was gearing up to say that Vero was a portal. That would make Oo one of those

people that were able to locate her. It made sense in an irrational, magical way.

Plesu continued, "Stories tell of entire villages going through a portal to escape danger or to settle a new ocean. Vero, I believe that you have been sent to us to deliver our village. Oo prayed for a more permanent solution to our troubles and her praying brought you two together. Tell me, were you doing anything to cause you to vibrate? Meditating perhaps?"

Vero slowly nodded her head. Oo could tell that this made a bit of sense to her if you allowed your mind to wrap itself around the concept. With each level of explanation from Plesu, Oo could see Vero's countenance soften from fear to acceptance. At times, he could make out the beginnings of a smile from Vero. When Plesu began to describe that Vero was a portal, she continued to nod her head in agreement.

"Vero, I must plead for you to save our people. Will you be our portal?" Plesu asked. She mouthed the word yes and nodded her head one more time. It dawned upon Plesu and Oo at the same time that Vero did not understand what she was being asked to do. Vero did not just provide access to the portal like Oo did. She WAS the portal. This meant that in order for the village to use the gate, they would have to pass through her. One by one. Every villager. It would be like giving birth to each person in the tribe. Plesu began to explain what this would entail and Vero's countenance began to shift again. This time it went from the face of passive listening straight to a look of abject horror. She began to back away as the magnitude of what she was being asked to do started to dawn upon her. This was not a magic gesture and a wave of the hand. What Plesu was detailing would take work, concentration, and pain, with the pain mostly coming from Vero.

Apparently, the portal, Vero in this case, and the one who found it must start resonating at the same frequency. I meant that Oo would have to return to her prayer state and Vero to her meditative one. The spiritual vibrations open up a portal when the wavelengths start to resonate together. The stronger the bond, the wider the opening. Each person would have to go through the portal separately. The difficulty came from the fact that Vero was the portal and, even though humans were larger than Oo's people, Vero was still a small woman and the epicenter of the portal was her womb. It meant that Plesu's people would have to squeeze through an opening in proportion to Vero's physical size. The children would flow through without much discomfort, but the adults would make Vero feel like she was being stretched to her limit.

It was then that Oo realized Vero was their best hope but she had begun to reconsider her role in saving the village. With a quiet nod, she summoned her guards to restrain Vero. At once, dozens of the largest beings in the village converged on Vero, and in moments, she was immobilized, much to the surprise of Plesu.

"I will take it from here, Elder," Oo said calmly.

She turned and swam away to an open area in the ocean with the restrained Vero close behind. There was a pang of guilt that nagged Oo as she swam up to Vero. She herself had never been the mother to any youngling although, as leader, there was not a dearth of suitors. It was her leadership role that actually was the deterrent to spawning. The village was her child and its many residents were her surrogate children, but that was not the same as growing life inside of you. It was this lens that was coloring her emotions as she swam up to Vero.

The mysticism that Plesu had used to communicate with the three of them was still working in his absence. Vero could understand what Oo was saying, but Oo could not discern Vero's words. This suited Oo perfectly because there was nothing that Vero could say that would change what she knew she had to do next.

"Hello Vero," Oo began, "This has been quite an experience. With all the excitement, I never got to introduce myself. I am Oo and these are my people. We live for ten times longer than humans do and I am 250 years old. I have ruled these people for over 100 of those years. You have met Plesu and he is my most trusted advisor and my father's valued friend. He is 512 years old, although he hates to be reminded of it. My clan has been through a lot over the centuries; human wars, modernization and pollution, and scientific inventions. We have moved to avoid your people more times than we would like and we are running out of places that we can retreat to on our own. You can transport us to a place that we would never be able to reach. I can see the terror in your eyes and understand your fear. I, however, can not let that sway me, my new friend. We have been running from your kind for generations and it is time for humankind to be part of the solution.

I have to hold you here, Vero. If for nothing else than I don't know what will happen to you if you leave our presence, therefore, we can't let you leave. We don't know if the magic allowing you to live among us will disappear. And if it doesn't, you would starve before you found your way back to the surface. We are very well hidden and quite deep. Honestly though, your welfare is a low priority for me and the village. The chief reason you cannot leave is that mypeople need you and that glow you possess. I can not let you be the one to make that decision, even if it is your body. I hope you will forgive me for my use of force and eventually understand what you mean for our survival. You have my word that I will not leave your side. We are in this together even if our levels of freedom are different. You have my deepest apologies."

With that, she waved her hand and more villagers appeared with ocean vines that they used to anchor Vero to the main dome in the center of town. As Oo watched her instructions being carried out, the nagging pang of guilt took up more of her emotions and she questioned whether this decision was best for her people.

Chapter 11

"That's when I realized that they wanted to pass their entire village through my vagina!" Vero was telling her side of the story back on the dock in front of her friends and sister, and not one face was devoid of emotion. The majority of the faces were expressing disbelief. Patty's face was filled with sorrow. She had seen her clients have a total break with reality like this before but mostly it was with elderly patients and with far less imaginative detail. Her clients' lives were never the same and she dreaded a future like that for Vero.

Click's face was filled with wonder and she hung on Vero's every word. Click had been looking for answers her whole life. She was on her sixth religion. Born into Catholicism, mystical impregnation resonated with her even as she navigated the patriarchy of the religion. Once that became too much to bear, she moved to Buddhism, Hinduism, Orisha, and Zoroastrianism. Currently, she was studying with a shaman from the Wampanoag tribe, all in search of answers for the next plane of existence. When Vero started telling her story, Click found a new religion and Vero was its priestess. This was the proof that she had been searching for. This was her "Fatima of Lourdes" or "face of Christ on toast." This was tangible verification that what we can see with our eyes is but one version of the universe and that the stuff we don't know far outweighs the facts we do. If Click could shove everyone back into the house and have a one-on-one with her old roomie, she would start the Church of Vero right here and now. Since that wasn't an option, she craned her neck so that she didn't miss any detail. She needed to be accurate if she was going to be her first acolyte.

Vero continued, "It was the strangest thing. I was constrained by these sea vines but I never got hungry or thirsty. I just was. Every day Oo would come to me and sit with me for hours. She still couldn't understand my words but it didn't matter. It wasn't a dialogue. This was a series of monologues."

Indeed while Vero remained strapped to the village's main dome, Oo came by every single day. She would sit next to Vero and talk for hours. It started with a cursory inquiry as to whether Vero was experiencing discomfort, and when Vero shook her head no, Oo would start her daily diatribe.

The story was the same every single day, just a different part of it. It was the story of Oo's people. It was the story that her father had told her. That her uncle had told her when he passed the crown to her. That Plesu had told her. That all of the elders had told her. Now she was telling it to Vero. It was the story of explorers, journeys, migration of the tribe, heroes, and of survival. It began with the formation of the tribe, so many hundreds of years ago that it bordered on a fairytale in the retelling. Every day Oo moved the tribe and the story along for as long as she could until she grew weary and retired.

After seven days of this, Vero changed her answer to the question about her comfort level. She indicated that she was no longer at ease and that prompted Oo to retrieve Plesu to translate, begrudgingly. Plesu did not approve of Vero's confinement. He believed that the restraints were not conducive to her achieving the frequency of vibration that was going to be necessary to initiate and hold the portal open. Plesu believed that confining her in order to force her to help was going to have the opposite effect. The old man was not wrong. Incrementally, Vero's glow was starting to wane. He noticed this every evening from his balcony directly across from the dome where Vero was being imprisoned. When he was summoned, he assumed it was to discuss this diminished glow and was therefore extremely disappointed to simply play the role of translator. He did not sit on the High Chair so he did his leader's bidding without question and told Oo what Vero was saying.

"Why are you doing this to me," Plesu dictated.

"I told you. I cannot allow you to leave the vill…," Oo started to explain. Vero shook her head violently, interrupting Oo. Plesu continued to translate. "Every day you come here and give me the history of your people. You spend the entire day here and you miss no details. I am impressed that you know all of the details. But I don't understand why you are telling me this information. I am not joining your tribe. All I want to do is leave. I don't need this history lesson. In fact, I think I have forgotten most of it already. I don't understand." Oo sighed. After seven days, she wondered when Vero was going to ask about the reason for her daily lessons on Oo's tribe.

"We are asking you to do an incredibly hard thing. It is not lost on us that it comes at great sacrifice and with an enormous amount of pain. My people are desperate though and we have so very few choices. You are the solution that we prayed for. That I prayed for. However, it is no small feat for an entire village to pass through your portal. What we ask is monumental. No one does monumental things for people that they don't know. I have been sitting here, telling you the story of our people so that you will know who is asking you for this great sacrifice. I had hoped to pass our people through your mind and heart so you know who is asking to pass through your portal. Do you understand?"

She did. It worked. Vero understood their plight and her role in their salvation. This was the kind of act that all of the years of going to church had been preparing her for, and she didn't even realize it.

"If I do this, how will I know that I won't get sucked back into this when the tribe is in jeopardy again. Clearly, I will never do yoga again but how do I know that you will not try to summon me once more?

"I cannot answer that," Oo responded truthfully, to Vero's surprise. "I have gotten the full story of the portals from Plesu and to my understanding, you and I are connected, however, it is not the only connection that you or I can make. Another like me may be able to vibrate in sync with you and I may vibrate at a different frequency during my prayer and align with a different portal. It is very old magic and as we said, many of the details were lost to disbelief. I give you my word that I will not consciously attempt to reconnect with you. I cannot guarantee that this will never happen to you again. But I agree: I would stay away from "yoga" if that is what brought you to me!"

Chapter 12

"Vero. Hermana. You do realize how ridiculous this sounds? I don't know how to take this in."

Patty needed to recenter Vero. Her counselor hat had officially been thrown out and she was trying to connect with Vero on a friendship level. If she were convinced that Vero was still attached to the real world, then Patty could chalk it up to an elaborate and very detailed dream or meditative state. Where she had disappeared to would be a topic for another time. First things first: she had to ensure Vero was not delusional.

"I mean water princesses, underwater villages, portals coming out of your chocha. Take a step outside of yourself telling the story and imagine if you were hearing it from someone else. Wouldn't you have a hard time believing this?"

Vero paused her story for a few moments and considered what Patty had said.

"No, I get it. If I were hearing this from someone else, it would seem improbable at best, but since I actually experienced it, I know this is real. A whole village passed through my body to a different part of the world. It happened."

"Wait. You went through with it?" asked Click with the inquisitiveness of a kid at storytime at the local library. "I was betting that the next thing you told us was how you escaped!"

"No. I agreed to be their portal and it was the hardest thing I have ever done" That was probably the biggest understatement of her life. Women have given birth billions of times over the course of humanity, millions of them have given birth to more than one child at a time, but it was safe to say that few beings had birthed an entire village over the course of two weeks. But that was what Vero had done. She had indeed agreed to be the portal for Oo's village but on her terms. The linked women sat down the next day and organized a plan.

Judging from the pain that Vero experienced when Oo passed through her, she knew that she could not continue to meditate in a fashion that would keep the portal, her portal, open. They worked out a system where families would pass through one at a time, starting with the larger adults and working their way down to the children and infants. This allowed Vero to get past the more intense pain first, and ease into the end of the day with far fewer traumatic transitions. Each evening the village healers came by and soothed Vero's body with ointments and sea plants that Vero had never seen. Oo never left her side and as each villager passed through Vero, she gave her a brief history of their family and their role in the tribe. Even the little ones, narrated the hopes and wishes that their parents had for them. Once done, Vero rested and resumed this procedure the next day. This took two weeks to complete and on the last day, the only remaining members of the tribe were the healers, Plesu, and Oo.

Once the healers had passed through and Vero caught her breath, Plesu approached with a continence of reverence that is usually reserved for deities.

"Vero. There is no way of expressing the gratitude that my people have for you. There is no way that we can ever repay you for your sacrifice. There is also not one of us that will not remember you to our dying day. There is not one of us that will not tell the story of how you came to our village and saved us. To say that we owe you a debt that can never be repaid is an insult to those words. You will always be a part of our history and we hope that you will remember us. May the universe return to you tenfold what you have given to us and may you live out the rest of your days in joy and peace. Bless you, my child."

And with that, without waiting for a response he slipped through Vero's portal with the ease of a baby. It was as if he had channeled some new magic, so as to not be a further burden on her. With Plesu gone, Oo could only talk to Vero but after all this time in the village, she had picked up a few words from her people's savior. In a valiant effort to use English, Oo said, "Thank you, my friend." and she touched Vero's heart then mimicked the motion to her own heart. The two women touched their foreheads and said goodbye in a way that did not require words.

Oo passed through Vero's portal and there was a flash of light exactly like the one that had transported her here to begin with. Vero blinked her eyes and when she opened them, she was back on the dock and very disoriented. She stumbled around, being careful to not fall into the water. She had enough water for a VERY long time. As she got her land legs, everyone from her trip to Thailand came running out. She was back and the relief sapped all of the energy from her body, as she collapsed at Click's feet.

Immediately, it dawned on Vero that this was going to be a near-impossible story for her friends to grasp. She considered, for a moment, keeping the details to herself but she needed to know how long she was gone for. She knew just asking that question would spark a realization that something had happened to her. In a split-second decision, she decided to go with the truth.

Now here she was, telling that truth to her group, none of whom looked like they believed her. Except Click. After she finished her tale, she surveyed the crowd to see if she had any other believers besides Click. Not one of them seemed to be buying that Vero had transformed into some crazy stargate to another world. Patty was pacing and Vero was pretty sure she didn't realize that she was doing so. Connie looked annoyed that the attention was off of her again on a trip that was supposed to be a celebration of her birthday. Kwame was hovering, creeper style, and Vero was pretty sure that he tried to take a peek through the folds of the blankets covering her naked body. She made a mental note to stay far away from that one. Click was the only one who had a "tell me more" face.

With her quick assessment of the situation, Vero decided to give everyone an out so that they could go back to their trip.

"This all seemed so real but as I'm coming out of my fog, I might have hallucinated the entire thing. I think something we ate yesterday might have affected me strangely. It seemed so real though. I am sorry that I scared everyone. Click can you help me up?"

"Absolutely," she responded and stood up to help her friend. As she stood up, Vero leaned in and said,

"You believe me, don't you?"

Click nodded silently and helped her friend into the water house. They got her into new clothes and got her something to eat, all while everyone gave their version of the crazy events of the morning. Once breakfast was done, the locals took the group on an expedition on the river, but Vero and Click remained behind, citing exhaustion and disinterest respectively.

Neither of the women said a word as their friends departed for the day's activities. Once they were alone with only the host wife, Vero turned to Click and raised her shirt while lowering the tops of her pants, beckoning her to look at her midriff. Click leaned in. Ever so gently, the area of Vero's womb was pulsing and, almost indiscernible, glowing. Click gasped audibly and Vero quickly shushed her. They did not speak of it for the rest of the trip but they were inseparable.

After the trip was over, Click moved to New Jersey to be near Vero, a move that irritated Patty. Her job required her to travel quite a bit and it didn't really matter where her home base was. It seemed to reinvigorate Vero though and she and

Click spent every spare moment at libraries, religious houses, and self-proclaimed mystical places.

After months of this, and no answers to explain what had happened to Vero, they eased up on the exploration and settled back into some semblance of regular life.

The new best friends decided to take a girls' spa day after an especially tough work week for them both. They went to get a dual massage (Vero laughed out loud when the rep ushered them back for their couple's massage) and it was incredible. After it was completed, Click heard Vero moan in satisfaction as the masseuses walked out.

"That hit the spot for you, didn't it, Vero? Vero… VERO?!?!?"

Vero had disappeared.

PORTAL FUN FACTS

Here are some of the facts in Portal that you may not have known about:

- There is an actual floating village in Siem Reap, Cambodia. There are four villages on the Tonle Sap Lake.
  https://britonthemove.com/floating-villages-siem-reap/

- Esports arenas are very popular and the one in Vegas was a state of the art facility.
  https://blog.ggcircuit.com/hyperx-esports-arena-las-vegas-the-ultimate-guide

- Yogis instruct participants to focus on their chakras. One of the chakras is located in your genitalia. **https://en.wikipedia.org/wiki/Chakra**

CHAOS

Delta hated change.

She was never sure whether it was organic and a coincidence that her name was the mathematical symbol for change or whether she was opposed to it because of the name. Either way, she was a woman who appreciated consistency and regularity. She enjoyed a good sunset because she could predict exactly when the flaming ball would disappear below the horizon. Tides gave her comfort. Even the annoyance of the cacophony of the cicadas relaxed her because they, too, respected consistency and schedule. It was the primary driver for her career in science.

The ability to predict results based on previous experimentation was extremely attractive to her. Even new discoveries, albeit evidence of change, didn't phase her. Those new discoveries could be replicated with a measure of success and predictability. Serenity was found in a lab among the beakers, bunsen burners, and immutable results. It was where she found Xanadu.

Chuck envied and resented his friend's consistency. Linked since childhood, Chuck's mind simply did not work the same way. He enjoyed a new adventure and the universe knew this, serving up detour after detour on his life's path. The fault in Chuck's life was his decision-making. At every divergent path, Chuck seemed to pick the most difficult option. Wonderful stories to recant? Absolutely! Losses in time, money and relationships? Too many to recant as well. To add insult to injury, the universe poked fun at the few successes he did manage to scrape together. New job? The company would get shut down due to multiple SEC violations. His attempt to lose weight? He broke his foot on the second day of the workout routine.

The latest "gotcha" was that he finally decided to get clean from weed and booze. During his check-up, his doctor expressed a concern that he had not been checking his prostate. In proper Chuck fashion, the test was positive and it was bad. After a lifetime of smoking and drinking, both his lungs and liver were fine. It was his prostate that was going to take him out. Chuck was the poster child for the old line, "If not for bad luck, I would have none."

This was how he started the conversation with Delta at their regular monthly brunch. A testament to Delta's desire to keep things the same, they met on the first Sunday of every month. Even though their lives had long since gone in very different directions, she was adamant that she was going to maintain this childhood relationship. It was obvious that she was the glue in this pairing and that suited Delta just fine. Both she and Chuck had their roles to play in the bond and it would upset the balance if Chuck showed up with his life all sorted out.

"I'm dying," Chuck blurted out in between sips of coffee that was strong enough to walk over on its own power.

"We all are," Delta retorted, as she savored a bite of her favorite dessert, yellow cake and vanilla ice cream. "Scientifically, we start dying the moment we are born."

"Well, then I finally found something that I'm better at than you, old friend. But seriously, I'm very sick. They found the Big C."
Delta returned from the euphoria of her sweet treat and straightened up. This was serious news. It required the serious version of herself.

"Where? What stage?"

Her tone was now decidedly more clinical.

"Prostate. The stage is irrelevant. I haven't got long. Maybe months. I saw the doc soon after our last meal like you told me. You were right. If I had come in sooner, they may have caught it and I might have had a chance."

"Yeah, but I was talking about your damn liver! There was no way I could have known about your prostate!" exclaimed Delta.

She battled the feelings of vindication nestled in an "I told you so" against the newest change her friend now faced. She was also facing changes and of all of the unknowns, death was the solemn king. She never had a road map for death in her life. Pets, family, friends, hell…, fictional characters in her favorite shows. It was the most permanent of changes and therefore reserved the most morbid place of honor in Delta's mental cabinet of things she despised. And now it had come calling to her oldest friend and her stallworth of inconsistency.

"I've been doing some reading and..."
"Please don't tell me you've got some untested herbal remedy," interrupted Delta. "This is serious. We've got to find you the best medicine or clinical trial!"

"You're absolutely right, but you have the tense wrong. This was serious. Now? Well, it's just too late. I don't have any herbal cure. What I'm about to suggest is even wackier than that. First, I need you to accept that I have come to terms with this. This is new to you, but I have been dealing with this for a month. Hell! I even saw a counselor. I'm in the endgame now. It's either I live the time I have left and go out with a bang, or try a Hail Mary."

"You're not even Catholic," quipped Delta.

Chuck chuckled.

"I don't have time to explain what that phrase means but I need to tell you about what I found. Have you ever heard of a chaos cloud?"

Chuck began to give details about the phenomenon, whilst Delta's face changed from curiosity to utter disbelief. According to Chuck, a chaos cloud was almost literal: a swirling kinetic dervish that was the source of chaotic energy. To the naked eye, they appeared to be dust storms and as a result, they occurred mainly in deserts. The closest recording of one was reportedly from the Mojave desert. The people reporting these incidents ranged from Yale astrophysics professors to some dude who fell asleep on a bender and his mates left him in the wasteland. Despite the range of expertise, the reports shared an eerie similarity. Once you have gone through a cloud, three things could happen: you remain unchanged, you experience some remarkable transformation, or you die. Not subtly.

The rumor is that the Wasteland Weekend festival was a cover for CCCs (Chaos Cloud Chasers) to get close to them. Legend has it that the organizer of the festival was an overweight gamer with heart disease. She happened across a cloud and poof: her heart was perfect. As a bonus, suddenly she could play the guitar. Her bladder never worked the same again, and she needed to pee every 30 minutes, but such was the trade-off. Such was the nature of chaos. Every report of a cloud encounter that didn't result in a dud or death, spoke of the randomness of the change. The festival was an homage to the cloud and the organizer's love for the movie Mad Max.

The more Chuck talked, the more Delta wanted to halt this madness in its tracks. CCCs? A Mad Max festival as a cover for people looking for a disruptive cloud of suspect results? This was all too much. Too little logic was present in this conversation and the future made no promise of added sense.

In that moment, something clicked inside Delta. She has a chance in front of her. She could burden Chuck with her incessant need to solve this problem. She could overwhelm her consistently inconsistent friend with research and science and probably alienate him, seeking treatment that may fail to yield a cure. She could throw every scenario her highly structured brain could muster at this tragedy until she figured it out. If she succeeded, Chuck may be miserable, but he'd be alive.

Or she could listen to her friend who had clearly resigned to his fate. She could be his companion on this crazy hail to Mary, or whatever the phrase was, and enjoy the last days of a man whose good days had not been plentiful.

She chose the latter.

Within a matter of days, flights had been booked, accommodations had been made, and Delta's lab work had been put on pause. They were really doing this.

Delta had called Chuck as she was finalizing plans. She wanted to confirm and hear from his lips that this is how he wanted to spend his last days. This was the last day to cancel and there was no turning back after this. She wanted to be sure.

"Chuck. It's D. This is the last chance for me to change the arrangements. Are you sure you don't want to go to Tobago and relax while you wait this out? I have been there a couple of times and it's a wonderful place to ease into the end of your journey," Chuck responded. "I am drowning in the weight of the mediocrity of the results from my tireless efforts to achieve greatness. Give me this one last chance to be amazing."

It was the heaviest thing that Chuck had ever said to her and it immediately put an end to any doubts Delta had about this trip. In two weeks, they were on a plane to Edwards, California. Once they landed, the craziest seventy-two hours of Delta's life began. They were greeted at the baggage claim by someone dressed as an extra from the original Mad Max movie. When they went outside, there was a bus decked out in post-

apocalyptic splendor. And so it went on for the rest
of the trip. Cosplay. Themed drinks. Reenactments.
It was all too much for Delta. Strangely that very
excess stirred something in her that she quickly
dispelled as an unsettled tummy from the marginally
health code-compliant food. Chuck was loving it. He
was jumping into conversations left and right, waiting
to hear key phrases that his Reddit group of CCCs
told him to listen out for while there. Before long,
he was chatting with a woman dressed as Tina Turner's
character in Beyond Thunderdome behind a tent. A
suspicious exchange of money occurred and immediately
lowered any possibility that Delta had for there being
a modicum of reality to any of this. Chuck returned to
where they had been standing, completely beaming and
she returned her skepticism to the holster it had been
occupying when she agreed to make her friend happy.
Chuck had been given coordinates for a cloud that was
supposed to occur randomly out in the desert near their
camp.

The next morning, long before the night creatures
burrowed away to hide from the harsh sun, Chuck and
Delta headed out in a rented or borrowed, or stolen
jeep. In the short time they had been on this trip,
Delta had learned to not ask questions that she did not
want the answers to…like what's in this drink…or who
does this vehicle belong to?

After an hour out, Chuck said, "We're here," to which
Delta responded with the obligatory response to a
location statement when one is in the middle of a
desert, "Here where?"

There was no marker. The moon was full so you could
still see the rise and fall of the craggy landscape but
no distinguishable monument. Except for a dust storm
in the distance which wouldn't seem out of the ordinary
except for the sparks emanating from it. It had the
look of an active thundercloud at ground level.

They had found a Chaos Cloud.

Chuck was right. They did exist. Delta quickly did some scientific reckoning in her mind. She never actually believed that they would find a cloud. She was here to support Chuck. She was not a believer. Chuck was and that's all she needed to make the trip. So when she was now face to face with something that she could not explain, she put the occurrence through academic and scientific rigor. This was indeed a phenomenon that she had never witnessed nor had she read about. Its existence was not proof of the supernatural. Just the undocumented.

That said, this Cloud was clearly electrical and charged with some unknown energy. The summation of these facts and subsequent assessment may have been enough for a believer to point and shout, "Magic!" but Delta was a scientist. That's what drew her closer to the dervish-like energy ball. Here they were, believer and pragmatic scientist, marching steadily towards the source of their combined curiosity.

At the brink of the Cloud, they realized they were not alone. Dressed in a slate grey kaftan with flowing locks of a matching hue, stood an elderly man clutching an ornate walking stick. As Delta and Chuck approached, he acknowledged them and stepped directly into the swirling particles, arms outstretched, ready to receive his blessing or his fate. At first, his face seemed to be flooded with joy. The expression quickly switched to agony as Delta could see the sand ripping at his skin, tearing great figures to the bone.

Simultaneously, the sparks combined into tendrils of energy that coursed through the octogenarian's body. This was the least desirable of the three outcomes. He was dying. Right there, in front of them. He seemed too frail to exit the Cloud and within minutes, his body was being stripped down to a bleached skeleton like the ones you see in old westerns.

Delta, horrified, looked over at Chuck whose mouth was also agape. Then he did something that completely astounded her: he stepped forward. Delta reached forward and grabbed his arm.

"You saw what I just saw right?"

"Sure did. That was crazy but that was his lot in life. It's now time to see what lies ahead for me. Our paths are different. I have to believe that."

There was such resolve in his voice that Delta released his arm and followed his steps in silence. Together, they strode towards this embodiment of uncertainty. Chuck with eyes wide open. Delta, conflicted by fear and curiosity, eyes trained on her longtime companion, hopeful that this would not be the last time she saw him.

As the first bits of sand hit their faces, Delta paused her stride. Chuck did not. Without looking back, he stepped into the Cloud to accept his fate. Delta watched with horror as the same sequence that the elder before them had experienced, now played out on Chuck. Lightening-like strikes hit the back of his head. Sand started ripping at his flesh. Chuck fell to his knees and screamed. He wasn't being changed either. He was suffering the same fate.

That was all Delta needed to see. She was not going to sit by and watch her friend be reduced to a pile of bones and a skull because this electrical storm wasn't magic at all. She ran to her friend and grabbed him. Chuck turned to her in agony and gratitude with a scar-filled face. As she walked him out of the Cloud, a stream of energy attached itself to the back of her head as well. Delta braced herself for the pain the two men before her had experienced. The pain never came. Delta would later describe it as a harmonic jolt that rearranged her atoms in a fundamental way. The strike felt like it gilded her out of the chaos and she dragged her friend's withered body to the edge of the dust storm. Once she reached the edge, she could feel the tether of charged particles dissipate. It was gone, but the sensation of the reorganization remained. There was no time to process this. Chuck was in bad shape. She had to get him to help now. She had tried his way and it had almost killed him.

This Chaos Cloud turned out to be a natural phenomenon, no different than a hot spring. Some people found them therapeutic, but some people found them to be no more theraputic than a hot bath. However, if you had heart problems, hot springs could kill you. The difference is that hot springs are well-known and monitored. This ground-level electrical storm was new. This proved to just be an untested danger. Now her friend was hurt and it was time for science to take over.
Delta managed to get Chuck in the back seat of the jeep of dubious origin. She hit the road and, as soon as service kicked back in, she navigated to the nearest hospital. "I knew you'd come in and get me," a weakened voice from the back seat said. "Oh my God. You're conscious. I'm taking you to a hospital."

"Good. I didn't want to die in the desert like that other dude. I know you didn't want that for me either."

"Stop talking. Conserve your energy. You're in pretty bad shape. I can't believe I let you talk me into trying some magic mumbo jumbo. You almost died out there. Hopefully, this hospital can save you."
"Correction. I can't be saved. If they can patch me up, cancer will take me the rest of the way. My ticket is already punched. I'm just glad that the Cloud actually worked. I'm glad I got to see it!"

"The only thing it worked at was ripping your skin off!" screamed Delta.

She got no response. Chuck had passed out again. Delta

hiked herself up in her seat to see if she could see the rise and fall of his chest and she noticed her eyes. Her right eye to be exact. It had changed from its former dark brown color to a new hazel tone. What new hell is this, she thought to herself and her musing was interrupted by a groan from her distressed passenger.

Right. The hospital. Time to floor it. Speed limits be damned.

When she arrived at the hospital, she careened into their ambulance bay. She pushed a dude with a GSW to get to a wheelchair. Bobbing and weaving through people with broken limbs facing the wrong direction and kids who shoved things into their ears, Delta hollered at nurses, orderlies, and doctors alike.

"I need a surgeon, STAT!"

Her background in science mixed with her addiction to medical dramas fashioned a vocabulary that halfway sounded official. Finally, a sympathetic nurse stopped her in her tracks and got more details. After what felt like arduous hours, Chuck was finally admitted, triaged, and headed to a surgeon's table. Even more hours later, Delta sat next to an unconscious Chuck in a recovery room. Groggily, he came out of his sedation and peered at her with thankful eyes. "Hey, old friend. How ya like me now?" waving his hands over the many bandages on his face. "You look like Two Face from Batman," replied Delta.

Chuck's eyes widened or at least the healthy one did.

"Well look at you with a Blerd reference. I'm impressed. I didn't think you'd ever seen a Batman movie."

"I haven't. I'm getting a doctor. You're slurring your words. You said 'blerd' instead of 'nerd'," and she stormed out of the recovery bay. Before Chuck could correct her, she was back with the doctor in tow.

"Hey, Mr. Howell," addressing Chuck, "Glad to see that you're awake. We need to talk though," and motioned towards Delta.

"She's more family than my relatives. She can hear what you have to say."

"OK. The wounds you came in here with were pretty serious, but not life-threatening. That said, your pre-existing condition is pretty serious but from your medical records, you already knew this. Unfortunately, this adventure made things worse. You put a lot of stress on your body."

As she listened to the surgeon, Delta slowly realized that Chuck's statement in the car was spot on. He was never leaving this building with breath in his lungs, and confirmation of this was coming from the doctor. His white coat was the latest in the line of people discussing his demise, which would end in a Second Line funeral procession. He had explicitly requested on the many calls, texts, and emails where they planned this trip that brought them to this very moment. Chuck took notice of Delta's facial expression.

"Are you mad at me, D?"

Delta's expression hardened but she tried to be soft with her words.

"Mad at you? Where do I even start? I'm sitting here in a desert hospital on a Thursday when I am supposed to be at "Wings and Trivia." I'm their science person and I know our winning streak is probably broken. I could start there. But I'd have to go further back. I could be mad at you for not going to a doctor more regularly. Or I could be mad at you for not letting me know that you were chasing greatness. My whole life you have been my friend who went with the flow and didn't care what lot life had doled out to him. I had no clue greatness was on your radar. This came as a shock to me because I could have helped. You know I don't like to shake things up so if you are a person who is content with an unencumbered life, then that's what I want for you. I have always taken you where you were. If you like it, I love it. But to hear that all these years you didn't like it makes me not love our history. I want you to be the greatest 'you', whatever that means for you. I am sad that I couldn't be there for you."

"Listen here, dummy."

It was Chuck's turn to wax poetic.

"If it weren't for your steady approach to life, I would have been in even worse shape. You were my North Star. You were the reason I even believed I could be great. Our lives are different because we are different people but that's just how the world works. You did help me. When I fell down, I knew I had to get back up so I could have my monthly meal with you. I would get nervous when we first started our tradition because I was such a screw-up but you never made me feel that way. Your consistent acceptance of me despite my flaws was what kept me going sometimes. I lived a good life. I had amazing highs and soul-crushing lows, but my center was always your love for me. My only wish when I was diagnosed was for you to have some highs in your life too. I knew that your acceptance of me was tainted with pity for my lack of success in life. My dirty secret is that I also pitied you a little. For all of your success, you have had very few memorable experiences. You don't have "Let me tell you about this one time when I …" stories. Those are just as valuable as degrees, D."

As he spoke, Delta tried to recall a crazy story to prove him wrong. She couldn't. He was right. For all her success, she had not lived her life to the fullest.

"That's why I am so happy that the Chaos Cloud worked. My recovery was secondary. I wanted the Cloud to work on you. And it was a success."

"Sir. Now I know you are delusional. That cloud did nothing for me," quipped Delta. Hours ago she had visited the bathroom to inspect her mismatched eyes. They had both returned to normal so she was convinced it was an optical illusion in the rearview mirror of the car. "Oh, but it did,' replied Chuck. "Perhaps not the Cloud itself, but this journey has been your "Aight…boom" story. You have been changed by this whole journey. That cloud was just the exclamation point. I got my wish and you have a story now. One of many future ones I hope."

Delta reminisced on the events of the last couple of weeks and they had indeed been atypical for her. Very atypical. Chuck had changed her right under her nose. She had been so focused on saving his life, she had missed the experiences as she was living them. She had randomly suspended her research, jumped on a plane that terrified her, landed in the desert, hung out with Mad Max enthusiasts, and run into a natural phenomenon that she just saw kill a man. Nothing about any of those things rang true for her.

"Very sneaky, Chuck."

He smiled. Then he choked. Then he grimaced. Then he passed out.

It was the last thing she said to his waking ears. He never regained consciousness. The next morning, Delta's treasured friend left this earthly plane of existence and joined the ancestors.

A staunch atheist, praying was not a thing that Delta did. However, with respect for Chuck's faith, she paid a visit to the hospital chapel. She issued a prayer

in the fashion she had seen others do, and headed out.
She was hungry and needed to eat. She planned to go
to the local diner and grab a commemorative meal with
her regular dessert. On her way out of the chapel, she
caught a glimpse of her face in the window and her eyes
were different colors again. She chalked it up to the
light of the stained glass.

Suddenly, she had a craving for tiramisu and rocky road
ice cream.

How strange.

Chaos Fun Facts

Here are some of the facts in Chaos that you may not have known about:

- There is a real festival celebrating all things Mad Max. It's called the Wasteland Weekend. **wastelandweekend.com**

- Dust Devils are real wind vortexes that can form in the desert. There are no information about any healing factors of Dust Devils. **tinyurl.com/AZDustDevil**

Sunday March 21th, 2021

Last night Friday Funk had an unprecedented night. The fact that he walked away from the Grammy ceremony with ten statuettes is only overshadowed by the fact that he won for songs in five different categories: Hip Hop, Pop, Country, Rock, and R&B. His latest album, Frankenstein, came out of nowhere and seems to summon the essence of every musical genre without pandering or oversampling. His music rings with authenticity as it harnesses the purest roots of each style. Normally artists dabble in different forms or two on an album, but this is something different. No guest appearances. No sampling of old standards. New music that somehow makes you remember the first time that you heard your favorite song from that style. Frankenstein is a collection of thirteen masterpieces that could have easily walked away with thirteen Grammys on Sunday. Friday won Best New Artist, Album, Record, and Song of the Year, Best Country and R&B Songs, as well as Best Performances in Rap, R&B, and Rock. It was truly a triumph for this breakthrough artist whose greatest achievement in music heretofore was a mediocre R&B offering. Knowing that this newest project would probably sweep through the Grammys, I scheduled a meeting with Friday for the day after the awards. Luckily, he honored our meeting and showed up, albeit bleary-eyed from a night of celebrating. Here is my interview with the new Golden Boy.

Rolling Stone: So how does it feel to wake up and be a record-breaking, Grammy Award-winning artist?
Friday Funk: I would have had to have gone to sleep first! It's kind of surreal. I know it's cliche but I'm just a kid from Brooklyn who grew up listening to all different kinds of music. I loved it all and this album was my tribute to music creation as a whole. I'm just happy that the academy saw and heard what I was trying to do.

RS: Let's talk about that. You mentioned listening to all types of music but musicians tend to have a singular voice. Your first album didn't have nearly as much acclaim and it was strictly R&B. A few years later, you produce this masterpiece spanning multiple genres. What happened?
FF: I think this album was always in me. I would listen to different songs and imagine how I would do them differently and better. When you start off as an artist, though, everyone from the producers to the A&Rs tells you that you have to pick a lane. I did that and it felt like a straightjacket. I decided I wanted to buck the system. I set out to make the best R&B song that I could. Then the best pop song. And I kept going until I had an Egyptian dozen. Hip Hop, rock, classical (he used air quotes here), Afrobeats, soca, everything I liked to listen to. I spent a year and a half just working on one song at a time then moving to the next one only when it was completely done. That's how we got "here."

RS: That's amazing. Do you recommend that format for new artists? Is your method the new standard or the bar?

FF: Oh hell no! I don't want to think that I broke the mold.
This worked for me. It may not work for others. Nor should it.
Some of my idols, M.J., Prince, Amy Winehouse, Cobain, and
Twitty, all slaughtered their genres. I'm not going to tell
anyone to do this. My ear is different. I'm different. Do you.

RS: That you are. So I know it's like asking a bride on their
wedding day about when they will have children, but what do
you do for an encore?
FF: I have no idea. This was my Magnus opus. I might pull an
Anita Baker and ride this out to retirement. Or maybe be like
Prince and keep making music and dump it into a vault. I just
hope that success doesn't go to my head and I end up like
Cobain. Honestly, I don't know. This is pretty hard to top.
Any suggestions? (he giggled)

RS: You got me! I'm just a music reporter. I hope you will
keep touring though. Speaking of which, I've been to your
concert. It's like the U.N. in there. Because there are so
many different kinds of music on the album, you draw a bunch
of different types of people. It's magical to see hard-core
rockers start to vibe on some R&B while a country dude starts
to sway to your high-brow operatic piece. Selfishly, I hope
you never stop touring. When you're on stage, are you taking
in what's happening in the audience?
FF: I wish I could say that I do, but I'm in the zone up
there. I can see the crowd, but it feels like an ocean of
people. The fact that they're all different people gets lost.
That said, I know that I reach a wide variety of people, so
I always assume and hope that my audience looks like my fan
base.

RS: Dope. Friday, I happen to know that Friday Funk is your
given, birth name. With a name like that, you must have deep
musical roots. You named a few of your influences, but tell me
about your early life. Were your parents musical?
FF: One was. Mom was a high school music teacher, so
instruments were always within reach. Dad was a business
lawyer. I had both the practical and artistic sides at home.
All my musical endeavors had to make sense, and possibly
dollars, to pass both of them. I know my dad wished that I
didn't go into music and would follow him into law. He'll
never say it, but he can't deny it. I hope he's proud of
how everything turned out. He seems happy, but you know how
Haitian parents are: you could be the pinnacle of your field,
but unless you're a lawyer or a doctor, they can't boast to
their friends about you! It's super weird. At least I'm on TV
so that's something, I guess. It's a small feather to put in
his cap.

RS: I have heard that about Haitian and Caribbean parents
as a whole. Well, thanks for talking to me, I hope to catch
your next concert. And thanks for making Frankenstein. It
definitely moved me. Go get some rest.
FF: Will do. Have an awesome day.

As Helen finished reading the Rolling Stone article about the man currently laying below her naked in a beachside cabana, she wondered if he had been entirely truthful with the reporter. Helen had known Friday for a decade, through his corny experimental years. He wallowed in self-doubt that a myriad of musical artists endure as they are starting out. Even as he snagged a deal with a minor label and put out his first album, he couldn't get his head together. Helen sang backup on some of the songs on that album and one of them even made it to the radio a couple of late nights on the R&B stations. The rest of the songs did modest streaming numbers and oddly, Friday had a small following in Japan and Germany. The label gave him an advance and the first thing Friday did was buy a condo in DUMBO that was a converted warehouse. He wanted a place where he could be loud as he played his music. Still, even with the space to practice and create constantly, his music was unfocused and banal at best. Then one day, as the crew was hanging on the couch, he stormed in and announced that he had found his muse. He grabbed Helen and kissed her passionately and then screamed, "Let's get to work!"

Helen and Friday had always been attracted to each other. They briefly dated but failed due to the cliche of music being Friday's first love and there not being much space for much else. She never left his side though. Helen loved him in a patient way. The kind of love that bides its time.

When he kissed her that day, she took it as a signal that her patience was going to be rewarded. Friday was by no means a catch. Broke, skinny, self-loathing musicians were a dime a dozen in New York City. But this was HER broke, skinny, self-loathing musician and she adored him. And he adored her. Secretly, all of the angst he experienced in his early years was borne out of frustration from the lack of success in his music. He wanted to be big so that he could properly take care of Helen. Archaic as it was, he valued being the provider for a woman and it sabotaged his ability to continue with their relationship.

Then came that fateful day. Helen saw confidence in Friday which was brand new. It was sexy. The kiss ignited her but the confidence fanned the flame. Whatever this new energy was, she was here for it.

That was the issue though. Musically speaking, Friday was totally different. He came into that living room from one of the weirder spots in the condo, the bedroom, proclaiming he had his muse. All of his friends inferred that he was talking about Helen since he planted a huge kiss on her right afterwards. Helen knew differently. She had done nothing to inspire him. They also weren't dating anymore. She wasn't currently collaborating with him on any musical projects. She barely chopped it up with him as of late. No. Whatever this muse was, he had found it in that corner of the apartment that she hated.

Friday's condo, being a refurbished warehouse, had many things in it that just didn't make sense…like an old potbelly furnace in the bedroom. The room's angles were all wonky because the architects were trying to be edgy. Even though Friday had been in the space for years by this time, there were a lot of spaces that were unused because they were so odd. The potbelly furnace sat in one of those odd spaces and it was the reason that Friday got a queen bed instead of a king. The fallow furnace sat in a strange location in the room that had a strange configuration, to begin with. Sharp angles. Sloping ceilings. None of it made sense… except for a quirky artist who had just signed his first record deal. Now the kitsch had worn off and Friday hated his bed and had set off to move the pot-bellied intruder in his room. After a few hours of that, he stormed out, made his declaration, and kissed his supposed inspirational figure.

Helen knew she was no muse. That furnace had more inspiration to give than she did.

At any rate, after that day Friday was like a man possessed. With a focus that was brand new, he attached a new song that would become the first single from Frankenstein. It was called "Work" and it was brilliant. It was layered and moody while still being upbeat. The lyrics were poetic and played with metaphors like the old great Marvin Gaye and the young Prince. He worked on nothing else but this song. Relentlessly.

Helen was enraptured. She all but moved in with Friday during this time. The energy was palpable and she wanted to be around Friday for whatever he needed. Need a sounding board for a lyric? Helen was there. Need a female voice for a part just to see how it sounded? Helen was there. Need a sandwich? Helen was there. Working on "Work" drew them closer than they had ever been before and pretty soon, they were inseparable.

Once they had worked through the song, it was time to go into the studio to record "Work." The musicians, singers, and Friday had been practicing this one song for weeks. Just that one song. They even demo-ed it at a couple of open mics to get honest feedback. It was a winner. After they laid the tracks, Friday and the engineer worked tirelessly on the song until it sounded exactly like he wanted. Some nights he would disappear into his bedroom and play the latest version on his laptop, and then he emerged with notes galore. Eventually, it was perfect. Helen felt like it was the best song she had heard in decades.

And then they never spoke about it ever again.

As soon as Friday got "Work" to the point where he was satisfied, he never played it again. It disappeared. The band never played it, nor did Friday play it on his computer for anyone. There were no more open mics. Poof. Gone.

In its place was a new song. Completely different genre. Country this time. The process for this new song was exactly how it had been for "Work:" hours in his bedroom, emerging with inspiration, followed by weeks of work on one song. This new song, "Buffalo," was so creative that it almost didn't feel like country but, at the same time, also sounded like what all country music should sound like going forward. When "Buffalo" was done, he locked it in the vault too.

Rinse and repeat for eleven more songs. A baker's dozen or an Egyptian dozen as Friday called it, citing the reverence of the number thirteen in Egyptology and pointing to hidden items numbering thirteen on a U.S. dollar. The studio begged for samples of what he was working on, but they were also infatuated with the mystery and intrigue of this new, secret project. They played along reluctantly, while hyping the release on social media for a year and a half.

Then came the payoff. After the thirteenth song was in the books, Friday obsessed about how to order them on the album and about which song would be released and when. It was painstakingly deliberate and intentional. They all felt like they were working on a Beyonce project. They hadn't signed an NDA, but the passion that Friday had was infectious and pretty soon they were all drinking the Kool-Aid. Helen was out front leading them and pouring heaping glasses of the metaphorical stuff.

Finally, he delivered a completed album to the execs and they set up a listening session for the rest of the label. Helen was at the session and holds to her claim that she saw one of the A&Rs cry. It was a religious experience. Nothing was the same after that. The label dumped a ton of money into the project and within weeks, Frankenstein was on everyone's lips; either singing the songs or talking about it. Friday was an overnight sensation, even though he had been around for years. Suddenly, he was in demand by everyone from late-night shows to the Grand Ole Opry. A tour was booked and the concerts were epic and revolutionary. All his dreams were coming true. At his side through all of it was Helen. Friday was loyal. He believed in dancing with whoever brought you and he never forgot his crew. He especially did not abandon the woman who had supported and stuck by him during his lean years. Friday still adored Helen and now he could finally treat her like he always wanted to. They moved in together and their relationship grew closer. Helen was swept up in it all. Suddenly she was in a different city every night. Fancy hotels took the place of DUMBO warehouse condos. It was a whirlwind existence, but she got to see a different Friday and that made her happy.

She couldn't help questioning what had changed though. It was too stark of conversion for her. Helen loved Friday's music before, but he was no musical genius back then.

There was never any delusion about that either. Friday knew he was a good musician and was just trying to make a living at his art. His highest aspiration was to be a touring musician who opened for Beyonce or Swift. With Frankenstein, he skyrocketed to their level and was in conversations as to whether he would be bigger than them.

Unimaginable was an understatement. Helen did not know where this savant-level acumen came from. It bothered her. A week after the Grammys, Helen, and Friday took a rare, non-music-related vacation to a super exclusive resort in Bali. It was there that the Rolling Stone edition with Friday's interview was delivered to them. Laying naked on a swinging platform on the beach, Helen read the article while laying on Friday's chest. It was peaceful. They had just had some edibles, a first for Friday, and they both felt super chill.

"Fri. Can I ask you something?"

"Anything. Although I can't vouch for my answers. I think I'm super high right now. But ask away, he replied, giggling.

"In the Rolling Stone interview," she asked, "you said this album was always in you. I've known you since the beginning. This project is totally outside of what you were creating. You also didn't talk about the eureka moment in DUMBO. I can't shake the feeling that something happened in the bedroom that day, but I don't know what it is."

"It's the potbelly furnace!" Friday said and started laughing hysterically.

"Wait. What?" Helen couldn't tell if he was making fun of her, or if the edibles were kicking in and taking over.

"The potbelly is a pocket universe."

"What?!?" Now Helen knew he was messing with her. "What the hell is a pocket universe, Friday? Stop playing with me. I was asking a serious question."

"And I'm being serious. I have a pocket universe in my bedroom."

With that, he promptly passed out in the face of a stunned Helen. Hours later, Friday woke up to Helen staring at him as the sun set on the beach.

"What the hell is a pocket universe?!" she screamed at him.

He winced and re-centered himself.

"Who told you about a pocket universe? Where did you hear about that?" sounding even more confused than Helen.

"You did! Don't tell me that was the edibles talking."

"Dammit. No more edibles for me. Apparently, I can't keep my mouth shut," he sighed.

"So are you going to tell me about the eureka moment or not?" Helen was beginning to get annoyed.

Friday sighed even more deeply.

"I guess it's time for you to know the truth. Can we get some clothes on, first though?"

"Fine, but I'm not letting this go. Don't dodge me."
Once they got back to their main room and got dressed in the bedroom, Helen stood in front of Friday on the bed with her hands akimbo.

"Spill it," she said.

"I have a pocket universe inside of the potbelly furnace in my bedroom and almost every great musician who ever died young lives inside of it."

Helen stared at Friday in disbelief and her face told of the pain that you feel when someone you love has lied to your face and expected you to believe it. She slapped him in frustration and stormed out of the room. He caught up with her in the suite's main living area. She was crying. "What was that for?" yelled Friday.

"You're hiding something. I am asking you straight questions and you're playing with me, talking about pocket universes and dead musicians," she yelled back through a wall of tears.

At that moment, Friday realized that dropping a statement about an alternate universe and missing musicians did sound completely ridiculous. He had never told anyone about this so he didn't have the right words to ease someone into the concept. He tried again though. "I was hiding a huge secret. This is that secret. Let me start from the beginning. Come back to the bedroom. And no more slapping!"

Reluctantly, Helen followed his lead and crawled into a ball on the bed at his feet like a cat. This was her comfort pose. She needed to settle her racing mind if she were going to wrap her brain around this madness. Friday began his story beginning with that fateful day in the DUMBO condo.

Friday had gone into his weirdly configured bedroom with the intent of moving stuff around to spark some new thought. He moved the bed, but the furnace was in such an awkward spot, it prevented him from placing the bed in a new position that made more sense. Friday figured the best solution would be to try to move the furnace. The chimney was no longer attached to the ceiling, so all he needed to do was get it moving. There were four other guys in the living room that day, but he needed to do this alone. The process was part of the experience. He pressed his back into the cast iron monstrosity and gave it a big heave with his legs. The front of the furnace tipped up, but the back did not budge. He stopped pushing and the front slammed back on the ground. That's when his life changed.

When Friday dropped the artifact, the force caused a door on the back to open. Unaware of its existence, Friday squeezed into the back to check out this new portal. As he squeezed into the tight space in the back, he peered into the newly opened door in disbelief. There was a whole city inside the potbelly furnace. There looked to be streets and buildings with people walking around. Friday leaned his head in to get a closer look and suddenly he was being sucked in. He landed on his back in the middle of a street, rolling away to narrowly avoid being hit by a car. A 1969 cherry red Corvette to be exact.

As he rolled to his stomach and watched the car that almost hit him go by, a man reached down to help him to his feet.

"Quite a fall you took there, fella. Can I help you up?"

His voice sounded familiar, but Friday couldn't place why it did. He dusted himself off and turned to look at the man who had helped him up.

It was Jimi Hendrix.

Not an impersonator, and definitely not a doppelganger.

It was THE Jimi Hendrix.

Friday stumbled backward and fell into the street that Hendrix had just picked him up from when almost got hit by the corvette.

"Ok. Take it easy," Hendrix was talking again. "Looks like you showed up here by accident. Do you know who I am?"

Friday nodded. Hendrix looked exactly like he did in the 60's. It was over fifty years since his death, but it looked like he hadn't even aged. Friday was convinced that he had died. The furnace must have fallen on him and killed him and this must be the afterlife. Jimi was speaking again.

"Ok. So if you know who I am then you know that you're in a special place. I happen to know who you are. You're Friday Funk right?"

Friday nodded, still groggy from all this new information and the fact that JIMI HENDRIX knew who he was.

"Now that's got to be the grooviest name I've ever heard. Is that a stage name or are you a product of Mr. & Mrs. Funk?"

"That's my real name sir," Friday was still in shock. He was talking to a rock legend. How? He needed answers.

"I'm sorry, Mr. Hendrix…"

"Ain't no Mr. here, brother! It's Jimi," Hendrix interrupted.

"Errr…ok. Jimi. So where am I? What is this place? You died five decades ago so how are you here? Am I dead too? How do you know my name? I'm so confused."

"I was confused when I first got here too. You ain't dead though. You're in what they call a pocket universe. It's trippy. I'll walk you through it, but let's not do that out here in the middle of the street. You drink coffee, brother?"

They picked themselves up and walked to the diner down the block. Friday looked around, but as far as he could tell, this seemed to be a normal suburban town, complete with a "main street." The only real difference was that this town had a very alive and youthful Jimi Hendrix.

They sat down in the window booth at the diner and Hendrix ordered breakfast for himself and coffee for Friday. Friday's stomach was in turmoil so he declined Jimi's offer of real food. Coffee would suffice for now.

"Ok, Friday Funk. Let me tell you the story of Pocket."

"Wait. That's the name? Pocket? A bit on the nose, don't you think?" Friday teased. Hendrix glared at him and Friday quickly realized that this may not be the right time for snarkiness.

"My bad, sir. Please continue," Friday apologized.

"In 1969, I was at the height of my popularity. After I played Woodstock, I felt like I was on top of the world. As a result, the whole world was knocking at my door. Every day. Every moment. Every place. I was partying and playing. That's it. My body was getting messed up because eating right and sleeping properly wasn't part of the equation. It was bad and I needed a break. One day, me and the crew were partying in Studio 54 and I tripped and fell into one of the bathroom stalls. I must have hit a lever or a button, but a tiny door opened up behind the toilet. I peeked in and saw this quiet town. First, I thought that this is the highest I have ever been because I must be hallucinating. I stuck my hand in to see if it was real and it sucked me right inside. Before I knew what was happening, I landed on the street right behind this one. Just like you."

Friday nodded, realizing the same thing had happened to him more or less, and Hendrix went on to describe how a man had also helped him to his feet. Dazed and confused, he looked up and realized that it was his old "frienemy," Sam Cooke.

Pocket was an alternative universe that existed in a parallel timeline. Pocket was just as normal to people from Friday's world except for one quirk: when people from this side of the universe crossed over into Pocket, they stopped aging. Kinda like vampires. Everyone else in Pocket, lived normal, expendable lives…except for a handful of interlopers from Earth proper. There were less than a dozen of them and they had all gotten there by one of the many portals that crossed the barrier between the two worlds. A few had stumbled onto the portals. Recently, though, there were residents of Pocket that were there by special invitation.

When Hendrix showed up in Portal, he realized that this was the answer to his burnout issue. This could be his retirement home. He devised a plan to fake his death and live forever in Pocket. It was actually Cooke's plan. That's what he had done.

Sam Cooke was shot in a motel in California in 1964. Jimi cried about losing a great singer and an advocate for musicians owning the rights to their own music. More importantly, he cried for his friend. When Sam picked Jimi up on the street that first day in Pocket, he knew that had to be dead because he knew Sam had died almost a decade before.

Sam reassured him that he wasn't dead…neither of them. Sam had found a portal behind a sound panel he was tinkering with at his SAR Records studio. Sam was making ripples that were going to become waves in the civil rights movement. He was organizing protests and boycotting segregated concert audiences. He started wearing his hair naturally to celebrate his Blackness. More importantly, SAR Records was poised to be the home for Black artists which would leave the major labels at a deficit for the talent that they had relied on for decades. He was unabashed about his culture. He could feel the walls closing in on him. Finding the portal was a godsend.

Sam was never in the Hacienda Motel. He never tried to rape a Hollywood prostitute. He was never shot. Alan Klein, Sam's business partner, was tipped off to an FBI scheme to drug Sam, set him up, and have him murdered. Alan and Sam devised a plan to find a replacement for Cooke. They found a guy that was a repeat offender and looked just like Sam. They paid off his girlfriend and son handsomely and then made the switch. The guy's name was Augie Howell Jr., but when they put the singer's clothes on him, he was Sam Cooke. Back then, grainy TV images and glamour posters were all you had to go by, so it wasn't hard to fool the average layperson who didn't actually know Sam.

Another payoff to the coroner to falsify the autopsy record and they were home free. Sam made his way to Pocket where he has been ever since. After a year in Pocket, Sam wanted to see how the world had changed since his departure. It was then that he realized that time moved slower in Pocket. In the real world, he had only been "dead" for about one month!

This gave him an idea. He knew musicians that wanted to get out of the game. He would talk to the ones that were dangerously close to self-harm or those who rubbed some people the wrong way, or were getting up in age and Pocket could extend their lives. The goal was to have the best of the music world in Pocket. He didn't know what they were going to do with such a collective, but he knew it shouldn't be more than thirteen. Sam would use elaborate costumes and sneak into the real world. He still had contacts that knew that he had faked his own death and they could get him close to these inaccessible artists. The first person he targeted was Jimi. Sam had known Jimi when he was just a guitar player on the tour. They also dated the same woman named Lithofayne. Correction: they were both obsessed with Lithofayne. Through his many visits, he watched Jimi rise to fame and start to spiral out of control. He was the perfect candidate, but before he could approach him, Jimi stumbled onto a portal by himself. The universe is weird that way. Sam often wondered if Pocket was psychically attached to his thoughts and opened a portal near Jimi because it knew Sam wanted him here. He resigned to the notion that he may never know.

With Jimi in Pocket, Sam quickly told him about his plan and Jimi agreed. They faked Jimi's death in London, but neither of them could agree on who should be next. They argued back and forth about whether certain talents should be taken from the world early or if they would sort their stuff out in time for them to have a long career. That was always the issue. Who they would expose themselves to was tricky. If the artist said "no," then they now knew that both Sam Cooke and Jimi Hendrix were still alive. It was only a matter of time before information like that leaked to the public.

"Wait a minute!" interrupted Friday, "Is that why people keep thinking that Elvis is alive and there are all these Elvis spotting?"

Jimi laughed.

"Hell no," Jimi replied. "We both agreed that Elvis was nothing but a thief and that he had no original talent. No. Elvis isn't here. That said, he may not be dead either. I don't know the facts on that one, but if Pocket exists, it stands to reason that other universes exist too. Maybe he found one of his own. But he's definitely not here. Nah, the first cat we brought here was John Lennon in 1980. He was a visionary and he started talking about rights for all people. That's what got Martin killed and we saw the writing on the wall. But we were sloppy and Yoko was super nosey. We almost got caught swapping the bodies and we underestimated how much his fans dug him. It was a circus. We didn't get the nerve to bring someone new in until 1992 when we scooped up Prince. Now that cat was a steal."

"Ummm you might have your order mixed up. Prince died in 2016. I'm a huge fan and I'm stoked that he is here, but he was definitely alive in the 2000s," proclaimed Friday. "Nope," Hendrix retorted. "That was a huge cover-up that made our job easier. The label hired a Prince look-alike for Graffiti Bridge named William Rector and started using him as a stand-in at recording sessions. Obviously, that pissed the real Prince off and he started a war with the record company. Before long they pushed him out completely and Rector changed his name to a symbol to legally separate himself from Prince.

Meanwhile, the real Prince exiled himself to an island and plotted his return. That's when we got him and convinced him to come to Pocket in 1992. The guy that died in 2016 was Rector. Look it up. There is a whole conspiracy paper on the dark web that lays it all out, except for us bringing him to Pocket of course!" Friday blew out a deep sigh and sloughed back into his seat. In a matter of minutes, he had just found out that his idol was alive and well, but the man who he thought was his idol was actually an imposter! Everything after The Gold Experience album was some dude named Rector. It explained SO MUCH and made him so mad!

Jimi continued to chronicle who else they had brought to Pocket. There was Conway Twitty in 1993, Kurt Cobain in 1994, Biggie Smalls in 1997, Micheal Jackson in 2009, and Amy Winehouse in 2011. They once considered bringing Madonna over, but decided it was much more fun to watch her make the world twitch with her shenanigans.

Every discussion on who they would bring to Pocket started with one of them bringing up Lithofayne especially after she almost got busted with Sly from the Family Stone. They always agreed that with her it was more about obsession than her talent, so they both passed repeatedly. It didn't stop them from bringing her name up every time though.

So here was this world where MJ and Prince still live and Biggie and Conway Twitty are the best of friends. They all had the freedom to write and play as much as their heart desired. They even put on small concerts from time to time in different regions of Pocket. Once in a while, someone would pop back into the real world and drop off a song that they had been working on so their sounds continued to live on. That practice produced varied results. When a real-world artist got a song from a Pocket artist, it tended to be a hit if the real-world person knew how to make it their own.

Two problems always cropped up: if the real-world artist didn't put their own spin on it,it fell flat or if they did give it their interpretation, they were never able to follow up on that success and it ruined them. Either way, the Pocket crew was very careful when they did that because potentially they could see their work butchered or ruin the career of an artist that they had chosen.

The next thing that Hendrix told Funk threw him for a loop. The people of Pocket, real-world interlopers and natives, knew where the portals were. Whereas the natives couldn't cross over as the interlopers could, they could see the other side. Portals showed up in random spots, like a bathroom stall for Jimi, in a studio for Sam, or a bedroom for Friday. When they showed up in an individual's personal space, there was always the question as to whether that person had been chosen. Sometimes the person never finds the portal, but when they do, the question of destiny arises. This was the case for Friday. When portals existed in the musicians' personal space, the Pocket crew took notice. They never showed the gateway to the artist. They just waited to see if they discovered it on their own, all the while tracking the career of the artist. They definitely tracked Friday Funk. Conway Twitty laughed at his name when he was first brought up for discussion and Amy reminded him that his name was Twitty. Kurt Cobain made the case that he was just like him when he was younger before he found a voice. Kurt said Friday needed a voice. Biggie voted yes just because he was tired of having to explain Brooklyn culture to everyone and needed someone who just got it. It was Prince that turned the discussion on its head.

"What if we don't keep him here if he finds the portal," Prince offered. "What if we keep him in the real world and train him to be our vessel?"

All conversation ceased. The Pocket crew all loved their lives in this dimension, but each of them yearned to hear their music adored by millions. The draw wasn't strong enough to make them want to have a miraculous resurrection in the real world. It did pull at them periodically though, so this idea from Prince intrigued them greatly. They decided to start crafting their best work each working in their respective genres, but also drawing from the rest of the crew. This new project invigorated them, especially Amy Winehouse whose star had the shortest rise. They had rescued her from alcohol poisoning so she owed them her life. She felt like her career was cut short and she had so many songs still in her. Amy spearheaded this project, making sure the songs were at a certain level, even with the limited technology available in Pocket.

And then they waited.

By no means did they sit around doing nothing, but they had started to annoy Jimi and Sam with the constant check-ins. How was he doing? Was he staying healthy and away from drugs? Was he making any music of his own? Michael Jackson always wanted to know if he had gotten a pet for some reason. Amy was the most persistent. This was her baby. It blew Friday's mind to hear Jimi Hendrix tell him that he was the topic of discussion among greats like Kurt Cobain, Conway Twitty, and Biggie Smalls. All he wanted to do was meet them all and he expressed this to Jimi.

"Trust me: you're going to meet them all," Jimi said. "I'm sure the news has spread that you finally found the door and they'll be here pretty soon."

The next few days were a whirlwind. Amy showed up first, of course, pushed past Jimi, and started laying out what the next couple of days in Pocket would look like. She didn't even inquire as to whether Jimi had gotten a chance to ask Friday to work with them. It didn't matter. Friday's face belied his excitement. He was a go. Amy drove him to the apartment that had been set out for him and let him catch his breath before the parade of music all-stars began. One by one, the Pocket crew showed up in Friday's living room, and with each knock at the door, his eyes grew wider. By mid-evening, Friday was sitting in front of MJ, Prince, Amy, Twitty, Biggie, Cobain, Jimi, Lennon, and Sam. Then there was another knock on the door. Jimi stood up to get it and Sam stared at Friday's face. They had not told him about this last member of the group because both Sam and Jimi recognized when a man was a little obsessed with a woman. Friday was obsessed with this woman. Sadly, she died in 2001, long before he could meet her, but he was consumed by her story. He knew all the details of her life. He even wrote a paper in school surmising whether she would be as big as Beyonce if she had lived. Her presence could derail the entire project if Friday became distracted by her. It would be the chance of a lifetime for him to possibly be around, and dare he dream, with the woman of his fantasies. This is why Sam was focused on Friday Funk's facial reaction as Jimi opened the door.

Aaliyah walked into the room and Friday's jaw dropped.

She looked exactly like the poster that was hanging in his living room. She looked exactly like the album cover framed in his bedroom. She looked exactly like the image that popped up on his laptop when he played her album at least once a week.

Sam immediately knew this was a mistake and looked at Jimi, letting him know his feelings. Jimi shook his head as if to say that it would be alright and followed Aaliyah as she walked into the room.

"Hi. I'm Aa…"

"Aaliyah. I know," Friday interrupted breathily. "I'm convinced that this is really heaven now." Behind him, everyone laughed at Friday's schoolboy crush. The only people not laughing were Sam…and Friday. Friday never took his eyes off Aaliyah for fear that if he did, this would all go away. Eventually, he blinked and his brain realized that her existence was permanent.

As he regained his composure, Friday cleared his now dry throat. He turned to Jimi. "I don't get it. Why didn't you tell me about Aaliyah?"

"Because I knew you'd react like this. We snatched up Aaliyah in 2001 because we had to get her away from R. Kelly. That was going to end badly. The world has had a boner for her since then. Sorry Liyah," Jimi said while turning to Aaliyah. "No offense but you do know that you're like the Marilyn Monroe of the R&B world. Anyway, Friday. You're a tad bit obsessed and it was the one thing that we weren't sure that you would be able to work around. You have an incredible opportunity in front of you and you cannot be distracted. Also, you got a great lady in the real world. Don't mess things up with Helen because you met your crush. I'm saying all these things in front of Liyah because if this will be a problem, we'll send you back, dose you with peyote, and you'll think all of this was a dream. Are we solid??

"We're solid," Friday responded.

"Solid," confirmed Aaliyah.

Over the next few days, the Pocket crew walked Friday through the logistics of how this would work. One by one, Amy would introduce a song to him with the artist that wrote it. They would spend time making sure that he got all the nuances down and that all the phrasing was correct. Then they would go over the music, note by note, ensuring that the vocals matched each beat. Once they were confident that Friday had the song, they would send him back to the real world to fine-tune it with the available technology. They would go back and forth between Pocket and the real world, massaging the record until everyone in the Pocket Crew felt good about it. Fortunately, a few days in Pocket translated to a couple of hours in Brooklyn, so Friday could disappear into his room for a couple of hours and emerge with days of work.

It was brilliant and Friday returned to his bedroom after a few hours with renewed vigor and excitement. He planted a huge kiss on Helen, declared that he had found his muse, and called the band members that were not there. He began to work in earnest and his band was thrown off by this new energy, but it was hard to not get on board. Musicians like to be musicians. Especially if they are trying a new sound. This was the shot of adrenaline that his band needed and they were willing to skip past the questions about the origin of the new fire in Friday's gut.

For Helen, she never put those questions too far away. Like the rest of the band, she too was caught up in the whirlwind and the new chaos was enthralling to her. But she knew Friday…intimately. This was a whole new person. The tiger that used to lay next to her had changed his stripes and emerged as a lion. No matter how much she enjoyed this new phase, she was not going to be able to let go of the fact that she knew that people don't make that stark of a transformation without some form of a catalyst. She kept an eye out for evidence of new drug use. She checked his alcohol consumption. She monitored the garbage for prescription vials. Nothing. Nothing changed except his drive and his creativity. That and a weird interest in Conway Twitty. She assumed he was doing research for the country song that he was working on. The other new thing was a picture of Friday photoshopped next to Alliyah. Helen didn't find it too weird because Friday was obsessed with the singer. She often said she was happy that Alliyah wasn't still with us because Helen wouldn't stand a chance. Still, it was hard trying to live up to a ghost. This latest creation was a little cringy, but not out of the ordinary. Coming up empty for clues made Helen more suspicious, not less. She kept it to herself, however.

Until she read the Rolling Stone article.

Those questions came flooding back when she noticed the glaring omission of the seminal moment in Friday's story. She could no longer hold back and now she was sitting on a bed in Bali discussing pocket universes. Not how she thought this conversation would go.

"Friday," Helen whispered, "that has got to be the most fantastical story I have ever heard. The problem is that it explains everything. There is just one problem. If I do believe you, there is one question that I need answered. I have stood by you through thick and thin. Endured your lows and helped you celebrate your highs. I have played second fiddle to your music passion and now I play that role against your fame. Through it all I have loved you in a way that even one of your love songs can't describe. What I will not do, however, is do all of that and have another come swoop in and take my place in your heart. So my question is, that picture of you and Alliyah that you said was photoshopped; is that real?"

Friday looked a little bewildered. After a discussion about a journey to another universe filled with legendary rappers, soul singers, country artists, and rock stars, he had not expected that the first question that he would have to field would be about the picture of him and Alliyah in his loft. He had never seen Helen be jealous of anyone, pre or post-fame. She knew that he belonged to her and everything else was a distraction. They had even had a conversation one time about groupies and mistakes that they invited upon themselves. Helen said that she would be able to forgive a slip-up if she knew in her heart that Friday loved her. Don't make it a habit, she said, but as long as she could feel his love, forgiveness would follow. Wisely, Friday never tested that theory. It came as a shock to him then that the same person who put that "weekend pass" on the table was now asking about a picture with one of his musical idols.

"Yeah. That is an actual picture of me and Alliyah. You get why I told you it was photoshopped though. Right?"

"You're missing the point," Helen sighed. "You LOVE Prince. You know all of the lyrics to Biggie's songs. You once spent a summer trying the guitar riffs on Purple Haze. But you have Alliyah paraphernalia all over your space. You are obsessed with that woman. And when the opportunity to meet all of your idols arises, the only one that you take a picture of and bring it back is Alliyah. Where is the picture with everyone else? Where is the group picture? Step outside of yourself and look at that scenario objectively and tell me I'm buggin.' Wide-eyed, Friday blinked at the realization that he had screwed up in a major way and hadn't even realized it. The picture was just the surface and Helen had no clue how deep the rabbit hole went.

In Pocket, Alliyah was constantly around Friday. She was part of the team working on music. Like Winehouse, Alliyah's career was cut short before she could create a large catalog, so she was just as invested in the creation process as Amy was. She liked Friday's energy and his willingness to try new things. The two found themselves practicing and singing at each other for hours in the sessions, then going to get tea to soothe their throats. That was followed by dinners and late-night conversations.

As the weeks in Pocket went by, Alliyah and Friday became closer and closer friends. At least that's what Friday convinced himself that they were. There was a sitcom-like moment where they ended up face to face after laughing uproariously and did the "should-we-or-should-we-not-kiss" gaze into each other's eyes. Friday shook it off and reminded himself that he was committed to Helen. He told himself that Aaliyah was just messing with him. She didn't want to mess up the project by starting a relationship with Friday and risk having him decide to stay in Pocket. He also knew that she wasn't above satisfying her needs without strings attached. He left that interaction and course-corrected himself. Or so he thought.

He never actually pulled away from Aaliyah. In fact, they grew closer, fostering what Friday described to himself as a "big sister relationship." He also described it this way to Sam Cooke who had pulled him to the side to reiterate the original agreement concerning Alliyah. Sam had observed them getting chummy and had become concerned. In actuality, Sam and Aaliyah were very close in Pocket. He was adamant that they rescue her from the R. Kelly marriage because he saw her as a daughter. He treated her as such once she got here, taking her under his wing and nurturing her development like she was his own. The concern he expressed to Jimi about Friday and Aaliyah wasn't just about Friday's obsession. It also had to do with protecting his pseudo-daughter from a musician she should never get involved with in the first place. He didn't want her to end up being treated like he had treated Lithofayne. Sam pulled Friday to the side when he saw the same look in his eyes that he once had all those many decades ago. Love is beautiful, but obsession is its ugly cousin.

"We're just friends," Friday defended. "She's like my big sister."

"I've heard that before, kid," Sam replied. "Be true to your feelings or they will make a liar out of you, son."

Sitting on that bed in Bali, Friday realized that he had become a liar. The whole point of the Pocket project necessitated lying in the same way that it required all parties to be truthful to themselves and their music. Friday had not been honest with his feelings. He had deep conversations about music, love, life, and success with Alliyah. She was his confidant and sounding board. If he were being honest, he would have admitted that he had fallen in love with her in a deeper way than sibling love. When the reporter asked him what was next for him, images of the rest of his life being spent in Pocket danced in his head. It was the reason he couldn't give the reporter a real answer. Now Helen was asking him to be truthful. He owed it to her, even if it rocked the boat.

"You're not wrong Helen. If I'm being honest, I got closer to Aaliyah than anyone else there. She's special to me. But we never took it anywhere-physically. She is in my head though, But that's the only place because my heart is filled with love for you. I am not going to deny that I have love for Aaliyah, but I am committed to you and that is the only thing that matters. Have I ever treated you like I didn't love you?"

"You can't ask me that," Helen quivered, holding back tears again. "There have been many times where I felt invisible to you, but I knew that is the life of the mate of a musician, especially a driven one. I always chalked it up to your work, both before and after the album. Now I don't know if I can shake the feeling that those times that you seemed distant were because you were thinking about Aaliyah; a woman I thought I would never have to worry about during your waking hours. This is no small thing Friday. You get that, right?"

"Yeah. I get that. What now though?"

"You can't possibly expect me to answer that right now, can you," Helen asked, incredulously. "You drop a bomb on our garden and immediately want to know if we can still grow tomatoes? Come on dude. I will ask you this: You have worldwide acclaim, you've been mentored by the best from the past, and you have access to the best of the present. What would you do if I asked you to never return to Pocket? Don't answer that right now. I NEED you to spend time with your thoughts and answer me authentically."

With that, she stood up and started pulling clothes out of the drawers and putting them into her suitcase.

"Wait. What are you doing? Are you leaving?" Funk asked with a bewildered look on his face. "I'm going to see if they have another room. I need space to think and I can't do that laid up here next to you. Know this Friday,I love you more than I have ever loved any man and no matter what, I want the best for you. But I love myself and also want the best for me. I am also old enough to know when what is best for me may not be the thing that's best for you. I hope we both come out on top when this shakes out, but that can only happen if you make a real effort to look inside. Right now, though, I need my space."

With that, she finished packing and walked out of the cabana without another word.
Weeks went by and Friday returned to the Brooklyn loft. Since the Grammys, there were a slew of press junkets, concerts, and television appearances. He was even reading a few scripts for movies that his agent wanted him to cameo in with major movie stars. Even a script for a play based on the lyrics of one of his songs made its way to him. It was all very overwhelming, and he could barely string two thoughts together before someone else was asking for his attention. One person who made no requests for his attention was Helen. She had disappeared since Bali. He had asked her to check in with him when she returned stateside via text but outside of that, he had no idea where she was. It was now a month later, and he still had no answer to the question she posed as she walked

out the door of that cabana.

Part of Friday was mad that she was asking him to give up Pocket. Granted it was the first time that she had heard of the place, but from his story, it was clear that it was a special place to him. He pondered whether the place was more special to him than the woman was. Was the place special because of Aaliyah or could he be there and not be around her? Was that the real question that Helen was asking? Was his indecision in fact a decision itself? His whole world had plummeted into chaos as a result of those truth serum candies. No more edibles for me, he reflected in a brief respite from the madness.

In that brief moment of calm, he pondered whether he would have ever revealed his secret to Helen or anyone for that matter. Friday loved every moment of working on the album. The obvious rush of working with these legends was heightened by the acclaim he received. For Friday, the latter always felt a bit hollow, however. He would have loved to credit each Pocket Crew artist as a contributor on their individual songs to pay homage to the collaborative effort. Friday never liked taking credit for any part of the creative process that wasn't wholly a part of his efforts. The fact that there was no way to make it known that he worked with other people gnawed at him constantly. The main issue was he didn't know who he could trust. His bandmates were his closest friends, but he didn't trust any of them to not exploit the situation if he gave them such valuable information. His recognition of that gave him pause and made him re-evaluate how he defined friendship.

Then there was Helen.

Friday trusted Helen with his life. In fact, there had been times when Helen actually saved his life, both literally (pulling him back from stepping into traffic because he was distracted while talking on the phone) and figuratively (pulling him out of a bad mental place when he was trying to find his way in the early days). He knew Helen would never do anything to harm him. Yet, he kept this from her. What's worse, she found out by happenstance, and it reeked of secrecy and deception. Since Bali, he had done some soul-searching as to why things played out the way they did with him icing her out of the most important aspect of his life. Every answer pointed to one common factor: Aaliyah.

He could no longer lie to himself and pretend that he hadn't fallen in love with her. A love that was the manifestation of every fantasy that he had ever had about the songstress. Few among us have ever gotten the opportunity to live out a dream in that fashion and Friday was so enraptured by the opportunity, he had become blind to his own feelings. After a while, he committed to be blind no more.

Decisions would have to be made. None of those decisions would be easy for him or the parties involved. Could he love and be involved with more than one woman? Logistically, it could but could he spiritually handle that arrangement? Many have tried polyamory and failed as miserably as those who have succeeded. He could cut Pocket off and forge ahead alone. Helen was right: the year of mentorship had matured him and there were new songs bouncing around in his head that did not originate from the minds of a supposedly deceased singer. He could make it without Pocket, but he would want to say goodbye one last time if that were the decision. Aaliyah was not the only relationship that he had forged in Pocket and it would be painful to give up the friendships with people like Twitty, Biggie, and Amy. It was more than just a romantic decoupling: he would be losing mentors, like-minded allies, and buddies.

The final option was the riskiest of them all. He could choose Aaliyah. He could decide to forge a relationship with her and make a life together.

The complications associated with that were numerous, chief among them would be where Friday would live. He could be the latest "gone too soon" artist and move to Pocket or he could take extended vacations in Pocket with Aaliyah and return to the real world having disappeared for a week or two. It would mean that Helen would be gone forever and the mere thought of that made his soul ache in equal intensity to the excitement of the prospect of months spent at Aaliyah's side. The elephant in the room was that Friday did not know if Aaliyah felt the same way as him. It was entirely possible that she was having fun toying with him and had no intention of creating a life with Friday if the option was presented. He could blow up his life in the real world and end up alone in both universes. The indecision tormented him for weeks and then one day out of the blue, Helen reappeared. She texted him and asked to come by the loft to which Friday happily agreed. When she showed up, her face looked just as pained as it had when he last saw her in the cabana. Friday wondered if she had been this troubled since that time or if being in close proximity to Friday had made those feelings re-emerge. Either way, he wanted to hug her and bring joy to her face as he had always been able to do in the past. It was clear, though, that they were not in that space. He wondered if they would be able to get back to that energy.

"Hey Friday," she said coolly as she walked through the door when Friday opened it. "Hey, Helen. It's so good to see you. I have missed you so much.

"I know. I wish I could say that I missed you, but I needed to put you out of my mind for a minute and run around this world naked and free to see if I was enough for me. I did that and truthfully, if I felt like I missed you in that process, I wouldn't be here on our doorstep right now." Friday picked up on the use of "our" and a ray of hopefulness leaked onto his face. "I totally get that," he replied. "You want something to drink?"

"Nah," she said, making her way to the living room area. "I'm good. I have to admit. Seeing you after all this time is making me anxious all over again. Part of me wants to walk back out that door."

"And the other part?" he asked as they both sat down on facing armchairs. "The other part wants to know if you have thought about what I asked you in Bali." "I have. I've thought a lot about it."

Friday laid out how he saw his options while Helen listened attentively. He admitted that he had developed feelings for Aaliyah and Helen nodded as if she had already known that fact, which threw Friday off a bit. He expected that to be a bombshell and Helen acted as if he had declared that water was wet.
When he was finally done laying out his thought process, he looked up at Helen. "Well here is what I decided to do," he proclaimed.

"Hold on Friday," Helen interrupted. "You completely misunderstood the assignment. My question was what would you do if I asked you to give up Pocket? Know this: I have no intention of making that request. What I wanted you to consider was how it would feel for someone you love to give up part of their soul in order for their happiness over yours. What would it feel like to put aside a foundational part of your being for the sake of another human's well-being? Would you want to do that?"

Friday thought that he had finally wrapped his mind around what Helen had asked and now he was back to square one. His face could not hide his bewilderment. Helen picked up on that and continued to explain:

"When you told me about Pocket you destroyed the version of Friday Funk that I thought I knew and loved deeply. You were no longer the brutally honest and sincere musician from Brooklyn who finally made it. That would have been easy to ratify in my mind if at that moment I had not realized that my sole identity was "the woman who loves Friday Funk."

She held up air quotes at this last descriptor and now Friday's face was awash with confusion. "By telling me about Pocket," she continued, "and telling me the truth about that Aaliyah picture, you were asking me to give up the self-image that I had in order for you to be ok. I was the girlfriend of a kind and gentle man who loved art and music and was not capable of causing harm to those he loved. In that cabana, I was introduced to a man who could deceive me for years and justify it with fame and notoriety and the trappings that come with it. You changed my identity in one fell swoop and asked me to be alright with it. That jarred me into a space that I was unfamiliar with for years: being rudderless. That's why I left. I asked you to do some soul-searching while I did some of my own. I'm back now. I know who you are. And I know who I am absent of you. I've made peace with both of those things. I am willing to move forward with my life with or without you. Whether I stay or leave will depend on your decisions, but you have no ultimatums from me. Just know that whatever you decide will be based on what's best for Helen. Do you get me?"

"Whew…I get it."

Friday finally realized what she had been through and saw their entire relationship through a different lens. Multiple emotions were crowding his mind, but all he wanted to do was hug the woman that he could never stop loving.

"Can I hug you, Helen?"

"You will never not be able to do that Friday. Unless you have the cooties or something of course. I will always save space for you in my world regardless of whether you need it. Come take it when you want it. But know that when you feel the need to leave, I have many other rooms to play in and my joy will never be diminished by your absence again. If you can hug me knowing that, these arms are ready for your love."

Friday stood up, Helen did the same, and they hugged each other like souls reuniting. Friday began to cry which surprised Helen.

"Why the tears, Friday? We're good no matter what you decide to do."

"That's exactly why I'm crying. I don't deserve you, you know it, and yet here you stand. I know exactly what I have to do."

With that, he kissed her, headed to the bedroom, and closed the door behind him.

That was five years ago. Friday's star rose and plateaued. His fans clamored for another album because, in the music industry, you're only as good as your last song. He did release one more single though. He re-made the Aaliyah classic, "If Your Girl Only Knew" as a haunting self-admonition of his time in Pocket. It was a stripped-down version sung from the cheating party's point of view, with tear-inducing sincerity and passion. Critics lauded it, calling it so connected to the source material that it was as if Friday had actually known Aaliyah personally.

Helen knew it for what it was: Friday's way of apologizing and trying to make things right. Their relationship was different after that day back at his loft. He had made decisions that would change them forever. Change is good, however, Helen told herself as she forged forward with her man. When she considered all the other options that were available to her, moving on with Friday at her side was the one that made sense for her.

After all, everybody needs a little Funk in their lives.

Hers always came on Friday.

friday funk fun facts

Here are some of the facts in Friday Funk that you may not have known about:

- Lithofayne Pridgon is an actual person that was romantically linked to both Sam Cooke and Jimi Hendrix.
  tinyurl.com/lithofayne

- Sam Cooke was killed in a motel. All of the facts about SAR Records and Alan Klein are true.

- The Paisley Papers are a real conspiracy theory paper.
  prince.org/msg/7/304202

Chance Encounters

CHAPTER ONE

Morning.

Last night was poetic.

Naked arms reached over more naked arms trying to embrace the
fleeting moments left in their slumber. He pulled the cover back to peek
at the body lying next to him wearing a fiery pair of heels...and nothing
else. There were more accessories and garments at the beginning of
the night but, one by one, they were dispatched after each carnal act of
the night. Only the shoes remained, purposefully. It turned him on to
see her tamarind-colored body devoid of visual interruptions or flaws,
for that matter, standing in front of him in a pair of crimson stilettos.
She could tell that he liked what he saw, so she left them on...all night.
Masterfully. They burned a hole in the fabric of decency last night.
The heels prompted acts for which they hadn't created a movie rating
category yet. It was filled with firsts, lasts, and corrections of failed
attempts of lesser skilled partners in their past. It was exhausting and, in
the end, she was so spent that she did the unthinkable: she didn't bother
removing the shoes. Her mind weighed the options of expending energy
to reach down and un-strap ruby catalysts of seduction against simply
collapsing in minor discomfort and removing them later. Sunbeams
indicated which she had chosen, and he smiled in recognition and
confirmation of his handy work. He enjoyed her and the extensive sexual
vocabulary that she brought to this room. Granted her vocabulary didn't
match the lexicon in his back pocket, but it was fun watching her flex her
knowledge while he flexed her leg in dynamic positions. He turned in
the opposite direction towards the nightstand where there was a clock,
a watch, a set of dog tags on a long chain with a wedding band, and a
lamp. He checked the time. 6:30 a.m. The day could wait a bit longer. He
decided that just as he had been awoken by a pillar of light, she should
be awoken by a pillar of arousal that he was now the proud owner of. He
reached over to where she was laying on her stomach and caressed her
tantalizingly curved back which produced a guttural moan from her.
He touched her at the beginning of the concave divot and then kissed

where his hand had just been, slowly moving down. In due course, his head was laying on her taut behind. Soon she and he would be covered in saliva, sweat, sunlight, and questions. Chief among those questions for him at this moment was her name. Even as he was sampling her morning delights in concert with her own early morning enjoyment of his protrusion into her world, he couldn't recall her name. Then, between a tongue trick that he had learned in college and him reaching down and releasing her from the bondage of the shoes, it came back to him...right in sync with her release on his tongue. Raleigh.

It was a beautiful name, and she was a beautiful woman. She was just not his woman. His name was Ernest Chance. Most called him E and some people called him Mr. Chance and mornings like these were becoming all too common, he mused to himself, mid-stroke. The thought neither altered his motion nor his future encounters. This is who he was...now. Everyone that dared to be a part of his life knew exactly what they were getting into when they went on a date with Ernest Chance: enjoy it while it lasted for it very seldom did.

CHAPTER TWO

Twenty-four hours before E re-dedicated himself to the exhaustion of Raleigh, he rose from the same bed with a sense of purpose. Today would be interesting in many ways and there would be nary a free moment. He relished these types of days where every minute was accounted for, and starting and finishing every activity on time was crucial or else it would cause a domino effect. This day would have him switching roles constantly which forced him to celebrate all the varying facets of his life.

His agenda started with a networking breakfast for young college men set up by his fraternity. E didn't get to participate in the alumni chapter as much as he would like, so he did his best to come out to events like this when his brothers asked for him to come. From there, he would head back to his office. E owned and operated a high-end event planning business in New York City named Maverick Productions, a name he used to have to defend during the Obama/McCain presidential campaign. E was a fan of the old James Gardner TV show and named his company after that. Since the elections, he found himself having to assuage emotions associated with Sarah Palin that the name evoked. In some circles, he presented the company as MP, Inc to avoid the backlash.

He was headed back to the office to pitch an event to a radio station to host their next award ceremony. This was E's strong point. He ran the company by himself with his "guy Friday," Forrest, but when he presented to clients, you would surmise that there was a staff of hundreds in his employ. Technically, there were. Ernest Chance was masterful in the art of networking and relationships. He knew that he could promise to have dozens of people at an event and feel confident that they would come through for him. He paid well, he gave reasonable amounts of tasks at each event, and, most importantly, he spoke to people with respect. No one ever felt like he was better than them, even though he signed their checks, which were always on time, as a rule. Mr. Chance, as his contracted employees always called him, was quite wealthy, but he did not come from money. He was a self-made man who was directed and focused and came out of college with his feet moving long before they hit the ground. He understood hard work and knew how it felt to not be rewarded for it. He always vowed to never treat his vendors and contractors the way that he had been treated in numerous jobs during his college years. For that one policy, he was well-respected, and people were extremely loyal to him. Much in the same way that a few politicians are known as a "man of the people," E was known as a "friend of the worker" and that reputation allowed him to make guarantees that he had no problem fulfilling.

His next stop was a mid-afternoon charity brunch for an organization called HerAdvocate, which provided legal services for women in abusive relationships at low or no cost. E enjoyed attending these events as a guest for a couple of reasons: firstly, he thought the organization was worthwhile and wanted to help, but secondly, it gave him a peek into what other people were doing with their events to learn from their successes or to not to repeat their mistakes. This particular event was low-key in terms of the scope, but not in terms of the attendees. The borough president was there, and he recognized the woman that ran Bloomberg's charitable endeavors. Of course, there were the normal hodgepodge of affluent pockets circulating around the main dining hall at Tavern at the Green, each pretending to be less wealthy than the next. This current climate made the rich feel guilty for their coffers, except when giving to these organizations. The event served its purpose which was to recommit some of the former donors who they had not received money from in the last year. HerAdvocate understood these were unsteady times. They still had a mission that they needed funding, so they set out to remind people that the organization was their favorite tax shelter. Good strategy and E visited their "giving tree" on the way out of the Tavern and onto Central Park West. By this time, it was 3:45 p.m. and he had fifteen minutes to make it up to Museum Mile to the Met.

He walked to the corner and hailed a cab headed downtown deliberately and got in quickly. A Black man catching a cab going uptown, even in the middle of the day, and even if the man is well-dressed, is still hit or miss in this city and E didn't feel like dealing with the feelings that having fellow humans zoom by him evoked. He'd rather pay the extra money caused by having the cab make an extra block to re-orient itself rather than stand on a corner and wonder whether he was a victim of racism, fear, inconvenience, misrepresentation, or all of the above.

Inside the Met, he arrived just in time for his 4:00 p.m. appointment and pulled up the order history on his iPhone as he walked towards Erica, his contact at the museum.

She was a handsome woman and looked like she made a lot of men do a double take in her day. She had the stately nature of a woman who had conquered all the insecurities of youth. Confidence flowed from her like the Ganges. Everything about her gait and her posture removed any preconceived notion anyone may have about pulling the wool over her steely eyes. E straightened up immediately; virtually and physically. He had emailed her previously, but this was the first occasion for them to meet and he knew that she wasn't the type of person that you could push around. E needed to be on point.

That was a truly sharp skill that Ernest Chance had honed over the years; he knew exactly how to relate to different people depending on the situation. Granted this was a business interaction, but E built a full character profile, adding a layer with every step that she took towards him. He was extremely adept at this for everyone, but he knew women. It was not uncommon for him to observe a woman for an extended period before approaching her initially. By the time he had uttered his first words, he already surmised what her reaction would be and what his next move should be. He moved rooks and knights around his mental game board like Kasparov and, most of the time, the target of his efforts didn't realize that they had been part of a master plan until he admitted to it. By then it was generally too late.

His meeting with Erica went smoothly and it gave him a bit of breathing room before he had to be back at 57th. Meeting with Erica invigorated him. She was sharp and decisive. After what he assumed to be years of dealing with the sexism of the art world and in business in general, Erica had adopted a very hard line when it came to her job, particularly with men. A high-ranking woman in the field battles the stigma of presenting as too masculine when she does things that men get praised for on a regular basis. Finding the balance between a more feminine leadership style, which is sorely needed in the business world, and the need for the old guard to have a bulldog is a tough mix for any woman climbing the ladder. A strong woman is far more fearsome than a man! Ask any lion! Erica was self-assured and challenging even in the limited arena and scope in which she and E interacted. E loved women who gave him a run for his money and from whom he could learn. Demure, subservient, and weak women bored him immensely. This was true for his business associates and his dates. As he walked out of the museum, he toyed with the idea of what a date with the older Erica would be like. Granted even though he had genuinely no interest in her, the date would be quite engaging.

That was still on his mind as he walked down the stairs from the museum and headed back to 57th Street to the last part of his day, an actual date with Raleigh. He whispered to himself the hope that the date was half as stimulating as the banter with Erica. He viewed that wish as reasonable, since Raleigh was an educator at Pace University downtown. She facilitated a social justice program at the school and was tightly wound. She was a true student of the "injustice anywhere is injustice everywhere" school of thought. Tonight, E planned to unwind her knot in a couple of different ways, starting with one of his favorite activities: massages. His favorite place was Aire Ancient Baths, and they took good care of him there, so he started the night with hot stone massages for them both followed by a cadre of other treatments for her while E got a shiatsu rub down. That experience would be followed by a relaxing dip in the pool of the Gansevoort Hotel and cocktails and then back to his well-appointed apartment in Williamsburg. His assistant Forrest had arranged for a personal chef to be waiting for them there, ready to prepare whatever they wanted to eat from an extensive menu.

That was Ernest Chance's style. He didn't go to the movies as a date; he arranged for a private showing with the director and some of the stars. He didn't go ice skating on a date; he arranged for a rink to be shut down and for you to get a lesson from an Olympic medalist in figure skating. Ernest Chance was over the top. Deliberately so. He grew up poor. The wealth did come until after college. He also grew up geeky and focused on academics, so not many girls looked his way. He dreamed of going on dates, but buried himself in his studies every time he realized the unlikeness of that happening. To make matters worse, he was a hopeless romantic, so when he dreamed of dates, they were extravagant. His imagination ran free and served him well all through college, where he majored in marketing. As he matured, his geekiness morphed into an intelligence that augmented the good looks that had developed over time. Now he was a well-read, intelligent, handsome man who took immaculate care of his body and was now a highly-desired candidate in a pool that most women described as paltry at best. And now he was wealthy. He had done very well for himself and now the only thing that he cared about outside of Maverick was materializing those fantasies from his youth. Raleigh would be a worthy participant in that tonight, he thought as she walked through the door. Tonight would be her encounter.

Let the games begin.

Maverick Productions was always quiet on Monday mornings. There were rarely events happening on Mondays. Clients hated meeting on Mondays because it took away from the time that they would rather spend catching up from the weekend. People spend the first part of their Mondays responding to questions from people who knew they weren't around after Friday. It is the instant gratification era where your customers have an inquiry on Saturday while grocery shopping, fire off

CHAPTER THREE

an email from their phone, and expect an answer at exactly 9:03 a.m. on Monday...and that's with a two minute grace period for you to get a cup of coffee. Response time was crucial in the business world these days when competitors were working remotely, generating a reply while tanning on the Jersey Shore. So, Mondays were not a great day for meetings.

They were however a great time for Ernest Chance and Forrest to debrief about the weekend. Most of the time, both E and Forrest were too tired to "break down" an event once it ends and they just headed to their respective homes with a head full of notes. Monday morning coffee was the perfect time for them to do a brain dump of the previous week's events: its successes and shortcomings alike. Both men were excellent at event deconstruction, and it was one of the strengths of the company. They never made the same mistake twice, and were always looking for ways to be better in their field. There was a real dedication to staying on the cutting edge and their reputation preceded them. These weekly debriefs were the source of that professionalism.

The other foundation of their success was that they had a genuine trust for each other and that came from an ease of communication that they shared which was unlike most male relationships. E and Forrest liked talking to each other. The Monday meetings were filled with conversations about Maverick events, but that did not preclude them from discussing the events of their own lives. Once they cleared the business, the two friends could spend hours talking about E's dates, politics, popular culture, or even sports. They bantered, argued, and sometimes cackled like old biddies! Their mutual friends teased them about their "bromance" all the time, but they were unfazed by the barbs. The benefits of a strong friendship in business were not lost on them.

In actuality though, Forrest was less unfazed than his boss. When the jabs came, he was always depicted as the submissive one in the imaginary relationship. Somehow, this always got under his skin even though there was no relationship to begin with. He constantly second-guessed his decision to come to work for E. People whispered behind his back that he was seduced by E's charm like his many women and that he wasn't living up to his potential. Sometimes they didn't whisper. They joked that E would never marry him and that he could do just as well on his own or with a partner on equal footing.

Forrest was brilliant and creative. In college, he was the go-to guy for ideas and leadership. He headed up multiple clubs and sat on various committees. He was the annoying kind of smart too. The kind where you want to hate him for being that much more intelligent than you, but still had an affable personality that ingratiated him to you. He was not loud or braggadocio. In fact, was quiet, considerate, and kind. He led with a kind of empathetic understanding of his constituents. But he was effective and well-respected. If they did superlatives in college as they do in high school, Forrest would have been voted most likely to succeed. And then E showed up. He was three years ahead of Forrest and they knew each other marginally while their college lives overlapped. It was at a homecoming event in Forrest's senior year which they both attended that E approached Forrest about coming to work for him in a new venture.

E had told a mutual friend that he had started an event planning company and it was growing. He needed someone to run the business while he built a client base. That friend reminded him about Forrest. Ironically, the intention of the referral was to bring him on as a partner. People felt that E used the fact that the economy wasn't in great shape to get Forrest to come on board as an employee, therefore, stifling his professional growth. Those were the whispers. They lodged themselves firmly in Forrest's subconscious. They laid the foundation for the doubt that he had about his decision to come work for Maverick. They were ever present when he worked on preparing E's elaborate dates.

That notwithstanding Forrest had great respect for E and his vision. He liked him as a colleague and as a man. His periods of doubt were far outnumbered by the times that he was very happy with his employment situation and his bank account. He may not be an equal partner at Maverick, but he had a great deal of responsibility, unfettered autonomy, and was paid handsomely. The one solace that Forrest always had was that he had far more disposable income than those people who were whispering about his seduction.

Forrest watched E slouched over the office couch as recanted a story about a party he went to this weekend. He had begun to think about his situation as he half listened to E talk about this bar with frosted glass bathroom stall doors. Apparently, people regularly have sex in them, and E walked in on two women going at it because they forgot to lock the door in their passionate haste. He vaguely heard E say that he refused an invitation to join them because, according to E, they were "sloppy drunk." Forrest wondered if E had any inkling of what he was thinking or how he sometimes felt. Probably not. That's not how Ernest Chance's mind worked. That's not to say that he was a selfish man. On the contrary, he was very considerate. However, he was on the opposite end of the spectrum when it came to being intrusive. He would never ask about your troubles or even think about them unless you invited him into that conversation. Once there, though, he was a more than adequate sounding board, but you had to get on his radar. Forrest had never brought up his misgivings and so he doubted that his employer knew they existed.

Forrest's ears perked up. E had transitioned. Often, something in his personal life gave E an idea that would be perfect for an event. This was one of them. Getting a peek at two women in a steamy bathroom stall gave him an idea for an adult photo booth that he could pitch to a lingerie company. Guests could come to the booth and change into the lingerie tops provided by the company and take steamy pictures as keepsakes from the party. It would be a perfect way for a company like Fredericks to get people to try on their stuff to encourage attendees to buy them.

Such was the flow of their debrief meetings: work inspired by play which then provided the means for more play...for one of them. As Forrest listened to the adventures of the man named Chance, he couldn't help but wish that he, himself, would go out more and have adventures of his own. Maybe this position had stifled something in him.

Forrest redirected his focus once more because E had begun to talk about this week's events. Back to work. Time to get serious, he thought. Ironically, Forrest had not stopped being serious.
It was three o'clock in the afternoon when E suggested that they take a coffee break. They had been plodding away nonstop and had ordered food so they could work through lunch. It was time for a break and people-watching on the streets of NYC with iced coffees would be a welcomed departure.

"So, whatever happened to that woman that you had me book the chef for? You haven't mentioned her at all today. Was she that blah or is it man code time?"
"Man code" was shorthand for the fact that men will dish the dirt about a woman except if he thinks that woman will become serious. In that case, you get no details about what goes on in the bedroom. Forrest secretly hoped that it was the latter. He would enjoy a reprieve from the date planning (even though it lined his pockets generously) but he wanted his friend to find happiness and move forward in his life with a woman that complimented him. That's what Forrest believed would make him happy.
"There was no challenge there," E responded. "There wasn't any pushback

on anything that I threw at her. Turns out, she was willing to fight for every cause except her own right to express her personality. I said jump and she was already in the air asking for my next instructions. I almost yawned in the middle of one of our conversations! Nice girl but not for me."

"Still looking to be fought with huh?" Forrest inquired. "We have enough arguments in the office, and you fight with clients all day? Why not enjoy someone who isn't disagreeable after hours?"

"I don't want someone to just disagree with me for argument's sake, but I do want someone who will call me on a statement or action that goes against what they believe. I don't want to be with someone who lets me roll over them. I need someone with fire in their gut!"

"Be careful," Forrest admonished. "The last time you had someone with fire in their gut, she turned out to be a dragon. That fire came up through her throat and nearly burned you alive..."

As they escaped his lips, Forrest regretted the words. E's countenance dropped and his eyes seemed to sadden in a melancholy way. It was too soon to talk about her. It had been over a decade, and it was still too soon. They could be old men rocking in chairs on a New Orleans porch and it would probably still be too soon.

"Sorry man," Forrest apologized, "I shouldn't have brought her up. But I also don't want you reliving those mistakes in search of excitement."

"I understand," E said, absolving his friend. "And don't sweat it. I barely think about India."

Forrest nodded in acceptance of the forgiveness and silent knowledge that E was lying about India. India was always on his mind, in some form or fashion but he was willing to let his friend deny it. When he was ready, he would come to terms with it.

"Anyway," E continued, "what...or who...did you get into this weekend?" "Not a thing!

After Saturday's event, I went straight home and..."

The conversation trailed off as the two men headed back to the office to close out the work day, blissfully unaware of the stormy clouds just over the horizon.

CHAPTER FOUR

Earnest Chance was well-read. He had read the classics like David Copperfield and the Iliad as well as some more recent works from Nneka Okafor. He read three newspapers every day and a half dozen trade magazines showed up at his office weekly for his perusal. He liked acquiring knowledge as much as he enjoyed collecting new memories. He loved to read, a love that was fostered during his geeky high school years.

But Earnest Chance had never read Moby Dick.

It just never made his list of required or desired readings. One wonders if he had been able to read the Melville classic, would he have been able to better understand India? In E's world, India was not merely a country with millions of captivating and alluring women; it was also the name of the one woman who wrapped him around her finger like a sari and had changed E's life in an incredibly tumultuous fashion. She was one half of a set of twins and E was on the debate team with her sister, Asia. Affectionately, he called them the Eastern Twins, but they were actually the Jenkins sisters. Asia and India were as divergent as two siblings could be and the irony of that was pounded home further by the fact that they were identical. Asia and E were on the same path in college: focused, motivated, and hard-working. India was the antithesis of all of that. Asia would have been a more realistic pairing for E back then but at that juncture in his life, E had gotten accustomed to women not being attracted to him that he didn't see her at all.

But he saw India. Initially, he didn't even know India existed, though. The conversations that he and Asia had very rarely crossed into the personal realm, and she never mentioned that she had a sister and definitely not that she had a doppelganger roaming the streets of New York. E met India quite by happenstance and he always said that he should write a book about how it happened. It involved a train, a bell, and a panhandler. To this day, it was the strangest, most pivotal day in his life, and it proved to be a catalyst for the man he became. That relationship was destined to end the way it did.

You see, Earnest Chance had never read Moby Dick.

If he had, maybe he would understand what happens to a man when he chases a white whale. Perhaps he would be able to recognize that he was showing the very same obsessive traits that Ahab had. Conceivably, E would have been able to realize when it was time to turn his ship around, count his losses, and move onto friendlier seas and less elusive catch. None of those lessons were learned because the man had never read the book, so the woman had wrecked his ship. It took him years to right himself but, when he did, he was stronger, wiser, and determined to not experience his India years ever again.

Maybe it was good that he never read Moby Dick.

Whether or not he had perused the pages was now irrelevant now though. He had moved on to calmer waters and was strong again. At least he thought he was. Right up until he saw the striking woman in a smart business suit sipping on a Manhattan at an event, looking quite annoyed that she was even there. Her aura screamed that there were a thousand collectives of universes that she would rather be than here. That did not deter the suitors, nor did it diminish the ferocity of their advances. He knew that face and he knew that aura: it was Asia, the more refined version of the Eastern Twins. After his trials and tribulations with India, he often wondered why he hadn't chosen Asia instead. She was much closer to his personality than the whirling dervish in human form that took him for a ride all those years ago. As he watched her from across the room, as was his norm, he realized that he had an opportunity to rectify that very situation.

In any other situation dating siblings would be an automatic taboo unless you're one of the Jenkins. But in this case, these were not sisters. Asia and India were so different in every fashion that they did not speak to each other. There was no commonality between them, and conversations were both strained and disingenuous. E had seen them interact once and they spent the entire time trying to be as contrary to each other as possible. The interaction ended with insults that would make death row lifers blush. As far as he knew, that was the last time they bothered to talk. He had no problem understanding why. When someone called your mother a whore, fully understanding that she was her mother too, there was room for conversation. The heart simply makes room for hate and despises the brain for its ability to retain memories of that person. There is no future. So, India was dead to Asia that day. They were no longer sisters, even though they shared a mother and a face.

He waited until the latest lothario finished his spiel and walked up to her. She was very well put together; polished, well-coiffed, with conservative make-up and jewelry. As he approached her, he couldn't help but compare how different she was from India. He neared her and she recognized him and smiled. Good, he said to himself, she's happy to see him.

"Still giving the guys a hard time, Asia?" he said, smiling back, "It's good to see you."

"Einstein," she replied calmly, "It's India."

Chance Encounters
Fun Facts

Here are some of the facts in Chance Encounters that you may not have known about:

- HerAdvocate is based on HerJustice which is a non-profit organization that provides services for women in battered relationships. **herjustice.org**

- There was a bar in NYC that had bathroom doors that frosted when you closed them. It was notorious for clandestine sexual encounters. **timeout.com/newyork/bars/bar-89-closed**

- Aire and Gavensport are real places that you can visit. **beaire.com/en/aire-ancient-baths-newyork#** **tinyurl.com/RTpool**